Cannolis and Casinos
Pelican Cove Cozy Mystery Book 17
Leena Clover

Copyright © Leena Clover, Author 2025

All rights reserved. No part of this publication may be reproduced, stored in a retrieval system, or transmitted, in any form, or by any means (electronic, mechanical, photocopying, recording or otherwise) without the prior written permission of the author.

This book is a work of fiction. Names, characters, places, organizations and incidents are either products of the author's imagination or used fictitiously. Any resemblance to actual events, places, organizations or persons, living or dead, is entirely coincidental.

Contents

1. Chapter 1 — 1
2. Chapter 2 — 10
3. Chapter 3 — 21
4. Chapter 4 — 28
5. Chapter 5 — 36
6. Chapter 6 — 45
7. Chapter 7 — 53
8. Chapter 8 — 62
9. Chapter 9 — 71
10. Chapter 10 — 80
11. Chapter 11 — 88
12. Chapter 12 — 98
13. Chapter 13 — 108

14. Chapter 14	117
15. Chapter 15	126
16. Chapter 16	135
17. Chapter 17	144
18. Chapter 18	154
19. Chapter 19	164
20. Chapter 20	174
21. Chapter 21	182
22. Chapter 22	192
23. Chapter 23	201
24. Chapter 24	211
25. Chapter 25	220
26. Chapter 26	229
27. Chapter 27	240
28. Chapter 28	248
29. Chapter 29	256
30. Epilogue	266
Chapter	272
Chapter	273

Chapter 1

Jenny King gazed at the endless ocean stretching before her, barely following the conversation at the table. It was high tide and the frothy waves of the Atlantic pounded the shore, receding with equal force. Warm sunlight bathed the deck of the Boardwalk Café but the breeze coming in from the ocean was cool, carrying the unmistakable tang of the salt water, mixed with a faint floral fragrance. March had arrived with spring on its heels and the locals welcomed the pleasant weather it brought. The island of Pelican Cove rarely experienced harsh winters and all the shop owners on Main Street were growing antsy from the prolonged lull, ready to kick off the new tourist season.

"Of course I'm going!" Betty Sue Morse's voice pierced through her thoughts. "Someone needs to keep an eye on these degenerates."

Her granddaughter laughed outright.

"That's a bit much, Grandma. Admit it. You can't wait to try your luck at the casino."

Jenny snapped out of her reverie and began to listen in. On the wrong side of eighty, her friend Betty Sue was a sharp poker player. She had been so vocal about her opposition for the new casino that Jenny had forgotten how much Betty Sue enjoyed a good game of cards.

"Can we call it a casino?" Molly argued, going for the literal meaning of the world. "The Lombardis maintain the Isabella is just a high end restaurant."

"Yes, on the Isabella," Betty Sue spat. "What kind of name is that, I ask? How can they choose that name, knowing the history of our island?"

Did she think they owned that name, Heather smirked. She had talked about it with Billy, her fiancée. There was no way the town could forbid anyone from using it.

"This will not end well," Betty Sue warned. "We all know what happened to the original Isabella. Why, the name is jinxed! Nothing good can come of this."

Jenny's aunt Star spoke up for the first time.

"Are you really that superstitious? I think it's exciting. The Isabella's history will bring more tourists. That can only benefit the town."

Betty Sue wasn't convinced. The upscale clientele the casino would attract were not the kind who would spend time strolling along the streets of a quaint small town.

Jenny marveled at all that had happened since winter. First, there was talk of a new restaurant. Blank forms had been placed at the library and grocery store, asking people a series of questions about their likes and dislikes when it came to eating out. The town committee had been bewildered since nobody had bought any new property, there was no construction and no license had been filed for a restaurant. Then a ship had sailed into the harbor one morning and anchored off the shore. A speedboat brought a group of people ashore, dressed in pricey designer clothes that had not come off the rack. The town of Pelican Cove came face to face with the Lombardi family.

Dario Lombardi, a short man in his late thirties with dark hair parted in the middle and inky eyes, stood in front of a packed town hall, holding a fat cigar in his hand. Most of them had been struck speechless. Flashing a thousand watt smile that actually looked menacing, he outlined his plans.

Jenny had stared at his presentation, her mouth hanging open. The Lombardis presented the Isabella, a luxury yacht or small ship, depending on your perspective. It could sleep a hundred guests in lavish staterooms, double the size of Jenny's home. There were two large swimming pools, hot tubs, library and a bunch of other venues to entertain the guests. But the highlight was their flagship restaurant. It would serve delicacies from across the world, along with the bass and oysters the Chesapeake was famous for.

"We'll have deep sea fishing, of course," Dario rattled. "Tours to the winery on the Eastern Shore. Everything the region has to offer."

He rubbed his hands when he flipped to the final slide.

"And that's not all. We'll offer a night life that will rival Atlantic City. Even Las Vegas."

A gasp traveled through the audience as the screen filled with a video of a dazzling casino, boasting roulette wheels and card tables.

"No slots, of course." He crooned. "The Isabella only caters to the one percent."

The murmurs that traveled across the room grew louder until Betty Sue pounded her gavel.

"Where did you come up with that name, young man?" she bellowed.

The ship was inspired by his grandmother.

"I bet that's a pack of lies!" A voice cried from the back of the room.

An old man in a wheelchair raised his hand, trying to be heard.

"Are you going to let these goons run through our town, Betty Sue? I say we don't allow them to bring this den of sin to our shores."

No one was surprised when the crowd erupted and the meeting had to be shut down. Some people vehemently opposed the casino while others could not care less. But the town was united in one thing. They hated the idea of a ship called Isabella.

The town of Pelican Cove had an interesting history. A Spanish ship called the Isabella had sunk off the shores a few hundred years ago in a raging storm. Despite many rescue attempts, several lives had been lost. Only a few people survived. They were brought ashore. Most of them never left, starting a new life on the barrier island that had offered them shelter.

"On this island, Isabella equals death," Jason had explained to Jenny later that night. "Superstition or not, that's the way it is. I don't see the locals getting on board with this."

Jenny believed anything on the ship was way outside the price range of the residents of town. As Dario Lombardi had explained, the ship would be anchored offshore. They did not need any permissions or licenses from the town. But he had offered to employ a few locals as a goodwill gesture. That stirred the interest of some of the youths but the older people squashed the idea.

"No son of mine is setting foot on that ship!" A man who worked at the fish market spat. He was a Survivor, the descendant of a sailor shipwrecked on the original Isabella.

His son had dropped out of college and did pretty much nothing as far as Jenny knew. She had hired him the previous summer but he had quit after two days, complaining of a twisted ankle.

The Lombardis sailed out of the meeting with a triumphant air. Betty Sue had huddled with her council members, trying to come up with a way to drive the new people away. They had still not come up with a solution.

"Hey Jenny! You look lost!"

A familiar voice brought Jenny back to the present.

"Captain Charlie?" she blinked, looking around the table. "When did you get here?"

"About five minutes ago," he chuckled. "That was some French Toast you made this morning, missy. Did I tell you I'm grateful?"

She waved off his thanks, assuring him it was her pleasure. The Boardwalk Café had closed for renovations a few weeks ago. Once they started gutting the kitchen, the contractors had come across one problem after another. The plumbing was bad and had to be replaced. There was mold in places and parts of the roof were rotten. The project had taken much longer than expected and was costing her a pretty penny. But Jenny was most worried about the inconvenience it caused her customers.

Captain Charlie came to her home, Seaview, for breakfast on most days. Jenny packed some meals for those who were infirm and drove out to deliver them herself. She had set up a temporary counter on the deck, with a limited menu she decided beforehand. Most customers came and picked up the brown bags, along with the coffee Jenny brewed at home and transported in big thermoses.

Her friends, the Magnolias, gathered on the deck every morning for coffee. They had all agreed it was the most essential part of their day and they were not going to miss it. So the women chatted and gossiped, ignoring all the chaos of the construction and the hammering going on around them.

"Why are you so chipper, Charlie?" Betty Sue boomed, a frown marring her face. "Counting your pennies already?"

"It's too good an opportunity to pass up." He grinned, used to her cantankerous behavior. "I am donating all the money I make from this venture to build a gym for the veterans."

A former Navy man himself, Captain Charlie did a lot of work to help rehabilitate those returning from war. Surely Betty Sue could not complain of the Lombardis' money being put to good use?

"Can't you do that with one boat, Charlie?" Betty Sue would not relent. "Word is you're buying a new one. They don't come cheap, do they?"

Captain Charlie nodded. Dario Lombardi had suggested he get a brand new boat, one that matched the splendor of the Isabella. He had even offered a loan.

"Don't do it!" Betty Sue warned. "The Lombardis will be outta here pretty soon, with their tail between their legs. And you'll be stuck."

Star surprised Jenny by agreeing with her friend.

"Not very loyal of you, Charlie. It's dirty money."

A hush fell over the group. Captain Charlie had an easy going manner but there was a limit to how many insults he would take. To Jenny's surprise, Charlie completely ignored her aunt.

"Harry Campbell over at the Steakhouse is not pleased," he addressed Jenny. "He feels you're encroaching on his ground."

Jenny bit back her guilt and defended herself.

"I won fair and square. The Lombardis held a blind tasting for the cannolis. They liked mine best."

Heather looked up from her phone, finally showing some emotion.

"When was this? Have you been keeping secrets from us, Jenny?"

"I did it on a lark. But they liked my pastries and asked me to design a whole menu for the party. Not the entire one, of course. Just a few dishes that highlight the best of the region."

The chefs on the ship would use Jenny's recipes. She had been asked to supervise them and be on hand in case of issues.

"So you sold out." Betty Sue whispered. "You too, Jenny? Why?"

Jenny waved a hand around her, trying hard not to take her disapproval to heart.

"The café's been closed for two months. You know the renovation cost a lot more than I thought." She pursed her lips in a pout. "It's hard, honest work and the Lombardis are paying me for it."

Heather clapped her hands, rolling her eyes.

"And why should you care how they earn it?"

They all asked her to shut up.

"Well, Harry thinks you are an upstart. I'd keep a sharp eye out in that kitchen if I were you." Captain Charlie warned.

Jenny waved off his concern. Harry Campbell was not going to jeopardize the party. He would not risk running foul of the Lombardis.

"So, ladies?" She glanced around the table. "You are all coming to the party, right?"

Betty Sue declared she wasn't going to miss it.

"What did I say, Jenny? Someone needs to keep these gangsters in line!"

Chapter 2

Jenny touched up her mascara in the vanity mirror, urging Jason to speed up.

"We can't be late."

"Relax," he urged. "You've been slaving on your feet all day, honey."

That didn't matter, Jenny argued. They needed to be back on the Isabella before the party started. She wanted to be present when the serving staff rolled out the canapes.

Jason stepped on the gas pedal and they were pulling up outside the small marina which was a pickup point for ferrying passengers to the ship. Jenny's frown deepened when she saw the crowd assembled. The line snaked past two blocks and comprised of the locals. Whatever their thoughts about the casino, it was clear the people of Pelican Cove had gone all out when it came to dressing up for the grand launch party.

The sun hung low in the west and the sky was a blaze of color. A cold wind had picked up, reminding them that spring was still tiptoeing in. Jenny had been sensible enough to wear a coat.

"Isn't she beautiful?" She gazed wide eyed at the majestic ship anchored a mile offshore, lit up like a Christmas tree. "Wait till we get on board."

Jenny had spent a large part of the day in the Isabella's kitchens, supervising the skilled staff. Actually, she had felt woefully inadequate among the Cordon Bleu and Michelin star chefs. They didn't need her watching over their shoulders and surely they could make better cannolis than her? But Dario Lombardi had insisted.

"You are famous, Miss Jenny! My mother is your biggest fan. Why do you think we chose this town out of all the others on the Eastern Shore? I wanted to be closer to Maryland but Mama put her foot down."

She wasn't gullible but she couldn't help blushing at the blatant adulation. So she had climbed aboard early that morning and focused on doing what she was hired to do. A steady stream of overnight guests had arrived through the day. The room stewards had been in and out of the kitchen, delivering steak and lobster to the celebrity guests. Jenny had been awed by some of the names she overheard the maids gossiping about – a pop star, a Broadway actress, a super model.

The ship itself was more opulent than she had imagined. But it was all very tasteful, unlike the garish ostentation she expected from the Lombardis. There were a couple of unavoidable mishaps in the kitchen and Jenny was late getting home. She barely had twenty minutes to get ready.

"You look gorgeous, honey!" Jason murmured in her ear. "And you shine brighter than a million lights."

"Don't be silly." Jenny blushed, leaning into her husband's comforting chest. "We'll never get there in time."

Jason took her arm and strode to the front of the line. Captain Charlie himself stood on the dock, helping passengers aboard. He blew on a whistle and told the first person in the line to step back.

"That's all for this trip."

He waved at Jenny and summoned them.

"Come on sweetie. I've saved a seat for you."

She and Jason jumped aboard, ignoring the protests that rose from the crowd. Two minutes later, they were speeding toward the Isabella.

"What about the others?" Jenny inquired after her friends.

Captain Charlie had ferried them across thirty minutes ago.

"And Betty Sue?" Jenny probed.

"Even that old curmudgeon," he winked. "And Billy."

The boat reached the ship soon. Young men in the ship's uniform were waiting to help them aboard. Red carpet had been laid in the aisles leading to the elevators. They rode up to the main deck and stepped out into a spacious area filled with a sizeable crowd.

Jason looked around, impressed. Tall crystal chandeliers sparkled like jewels. Waiters in spotless white shirts offered champagne and canapes. Jenny picked up a flute of bubbly and took a sip.

"Only the best." She sighed. "Dario hasn't spared any expense."

Jason popped a crab puff in his mouth and took a sip from his glass.

"This is the pricey stuff alright. I'm surprised they are offering it to everyone."

Jenny pointed out a couple of celebrities. It would have been hard to selectively serve them in the crowd. Jason admitted he had no idea who some of them were.

"Nick told me these people are A listers. Wait, is that …?"

Her ex-husband was in his element, shaking hands, slapping people on the back. Heather stood next to him, sipping a cocktail, nodding and smiling at the people he greeted.

"Billy's in heaven," Jason remarked. "Do you think he misses his old life?"

A hotshot DC lawyer for decades, Billy had suddenly decided to take it slow and moved to Pelican Cove. There had been a turbulent period when he dumped Jenny for a younger woman. But Jenny bounced right back after a brief reprieve.

She had built a new life for herself in Pelican Cove. And she had forgiven Billy. The two stayed on friendly terms. Billy had fallen in love with the Eastern Shore. Then he fell for Heather. The two were recently engaged after a long courtship.

"I don't think so but a leopard can't change his spots. Schmoozing wealthy clients is second nature to him."

They greeted people they knew and noshed on finger food. There were dates stuffed with goat cheese, roasted fig morsels topped with feta, melon and prosciutto, fried wontons, mini caprese tomatoes on skewers and so on. Jenny lost count after a while, deciding to focus on tasting as many as possible.

A server came by with a tray of raw oysters. When she began to pick one up, he asked her to hold on and squeezed a wedge of lemon on top.

"Thanks." Jenny was about to put it in her mouth.

"Don't eat that!" Betty Sue cautioned, wagging a finger. "That's not from the bay."

Star and Molly accompanied her and were trying hard not to smile.

"Hello! Hello!" Jenny cried. "I've been looking all over for you."

Jason hugged each of the women and kissed Betty Sue on the cheek.

"You look outstanding!" he beamed. "All of you look very beautiful tonight."

His attempt at distraction failed. Star explained why Betty Sue was miffed. Hadn't the Lombardis promised they would use the best of the local seafood, thus boosting business?

Jenny urged her to calm down and enjoy herself.

"Try the fruit skewers or the mango glazed chicken. It's made from Thai mangoes and is just divine!"

Molly pitched in. The town could take Dario to task later. Why not enjoy all the delicious free food and have a nice time?

"There's no free meal in this world," Betty Sue huffed. "I thought you, at least, would be smart enough to know that, Molly."

Jason insisted they sit and ushered the older ladies to a table occupied by a few locals.

"Howdy Jenny." Peter Wilson greeted. "Quite a shindig, what?"

"You clean up nice." She complimented the local garage owner. "Why am I not surprised?"

"It's the Italian in me. We are born with charisma and style."

He wanted to know about the cannolis. If they were as good as his Nonna made, he would give Jenny a free oil change.

"Deal." She laughed. "But the cards are stacked against me. I'm never going to win against your Nonna."

Jason gently dug his elbow in her side.

"Is that our host?" he murmured. "Looks like he's coming this way."

Jenny whirled around and spotted Dario Lombardi a dozen or so feet away. He was chatting to an out of town guest but he caught her eye and waved. It did look like he was on his way to their table.

"That's him alright. Dario Lombardi, our host."

There was a thud and a stream of icy water rolled across the white linen table cloth, on her new designer shoes.

"You clumsy oaf!" Wilson's wife hissed. "Look what you've done." She took a napkin and bent down, trying to reach Jenny's feet. "Your poor shoes, Jenny!"

Wilson had managed to knock down a water glass, causing the accident.

"I'm sorry Jenny." Beads of sweat appeared on his brow. "Let me do that, honey."

He disappeared under the table, holding his own napkin aloft. The table cloth was still dripping and Jenny stepped away, hoping to avoid any more damage.

Dario Lombardi had reached them and he was pumping Jason's hand, flashing his crooked smile.

"Your wife better deliver today. I've bragged about her food to the Senator. He's a big fan of the Eastern Shore. Has a weekend home on Onancock."

Jenny tensed but forced herself to smile.

"I just developed the recipes, Dario. Your excellent chefs will make sure the food is up to standard."

Presentation was important and Jenny was sure the talented staff he hired would make her homely food look fancy enough.

"They better." Dario stretched his mouth, revealing a gap tooth. "Or the old man will make you walk the plank."

Jenny was speechless. And so was everyone else around her.

"He was kidding, right? Of course he was." Molly muttered as he left them.

Betty Sue chose that moment to point out why she had not wanted the Lombardis anywhere near the town.

"They shoot people, don't they?" she boomed. "But you're a good swimmer. Captain Charlie will pick you up in his boat and get you home."

Jason put an arm around her shoulder and glared at the older woman. Jenny clutched him, unable to stop the shiver that ran through her body from head to toe. Wilson had resurfaced and was nodding his head in agreement.

Betty Sue surprised them by bursting into laughter.

"The look on your face, Jenny. That boy there is a child, playing at being grown up. He wants his old man's respect. Even if the chicken is dry and the cannolis burn, he'll never say a word."

Jenny crossed her fingers and hoped she was right. Half the table was wet and Jason led her away, grabbing a fresh glass of bubbly from a waiter.

"I better check the cannolis. Why don't you hang around with Billy for a while?"

He gave her a quick peck and told her to relax. Dario was trying to keep an upper hand or he had a sick sense of humor.

"Look around you, honey. This place is full of people who love your food. We won't let anything bad happen to you."

Jenny assured him she wasn't worried. But she couldn't shirk her responsibility.

"Be back in a jiffy."

She rushed to the edge of the room, trying to find her way to the elevators. Two steps later, she was accosted by Ada Newbury, the richest woman in Pelican Cove.

"Did you step in a puddle?" She gave Jenny a withering look, adopting her usual haughty demeanor. "You are a disaster waiting to happen, Jenny."

"Ms. Ada." Jenny greeted her. "Can I catch up with you later? I have to go meet the chef."

"That's right. You're the hired help."

Used to the woman's high handed manner, Jenny ignored the jibe. But Ada wasn't done.

"Really, you're a disgrace to Jason. Do you have any idea about the amount of collective wealth in this room? You should be by his side, helping him make new contacts to expand his business."

Jason was a lawyer, known for his brilliant mind and empathy toward his clients. He was well respected among his peers and had plenty of cases just by word of mouth.

Ada rolled her eyes, forcing Jenny to think big.

"See that man Dario is hobnobbing with? That tall, blue eyed man in the dark suit? That's Senator Logan Worth. His family hails from Boston. He's as blue blooded as they come. His father was a Senator, his grandfather was a Senator. In fact, they say ..."

Jenny held up her hand.

"You are too kind, Ms. Ada. You must know the Senator well. I won't mind if you introduce Jason to him."

Ada grew flustered.

"Well ... to be honest ... I don't know the man. Just read about him in a magazine. Actually, I had no idea he was associated with the Lombardis. No wonder they didn't have any problems with setting up this floating casino."

Jenny agreed and left the woman grumbling to herself. It was clear the Lombardi fortune attracted all kinds of powerful people.

Hours later, Jenny stood on the deck with Jason, surrounded by her friends. Dinner had been lavish as promised and everything had gone without a hitch. The cannolis were pronounced delicious. Wilson promised Jenny she had a free oil change coming.

"When can we get home?" Heather grumbled. "It's gonna take us ages to get a ride back to shore."

The sky lit up with a myriad of exploding lights. Dario had promised a spectacular fireworks show and he had fulfilled his promise. But where was he?

A few minutes ago, the Lombardis had popped a giant bottle of champagne and cut an eight foot tall cake to celebrate the occasion. Dario had not been among them. Jenny couldn't figure out why a flashy braggart like him was absent from the scene.

The fireworks stopped fifteen minutes later. Guests who were staying on board began to head to their rooms. The locals grew antsy, eager to get home. It was an hour before they all boarded Captain Charlie's boat and headed to land.

Heather held hands with Billy, a silly smile on her face.

"Aren't you glad you came, Grandma? Nothing happened!!"

Billy rubbed his head and laughed.

"All that stuff about the curse, just superstition."

The night was cold and they were drowsy from all the rich food they had imbibed. Betty Sue opened her eyes with a start and looked back at the ship.

"Laugh all you want, kids. I'm glad I will be sleeping in my own bed tonight."

Chapter 3

Jenny kept hitting the snooze button on her alarm the next morning. She finally pulled herself out of bed and stood under the shower, willing herself to wake up. At least she didn't have to drive to the café right away.

She went downstairs to her kitchen and glanced at the weekly menu pasted on the fridge. Jason and Star had both insisted she stick to one while the café was undergoing renovation. It had been circulated among her customers and they placed orders in advance about their preferences.

It didn't take her long to slide a large pan of banana walnut muffins into the oven. Then she began cracking eggs. Heather helped her deliver the food sometimes but Jenny figured she would be sleeping in that morning.

Her phone rang. It was her son, asking about the big party on the ship. Jenny rubbed the gold charms hanging around her neck on a chain as she talked to him, yawning her head off.

"I have to go now, Nicky. Already running late."

"Have you had a gallon of coffee yet, Mom?" he joked. "Don't fall asleep at the wheel."

Jenny hung up, thinking it was very possible given how sleepy she was. She packed the food in boxes based on the orders and set off. Half an hour later, she reached the Boardwalk Café and was greeted by the foreman overseeing the construction.

"Shouldn't be long now, Miss Jenny."

That's what he had been saying for the past three weeks so Jenny took it with a pinch of salt. She thanked him with a smile and promised to fix coffee for his men.

Jason and Billy had set up an old table on the deck since the renovation began. It served as a serving platform. The coffee and food were both limited and there was a line of people on the beach, waiting for her. Captain Charlie was one of them.

"I overslept." He admitted. "Can you spare a coffee and muffin for me, Jenny?"

"Of course! I can't let my favorite customer go hungry."

"What about us?" the woman behind him demanded. "I dragged myself out of bed and rushed here so I wouldn't miss breakfast."

Jenny sized up the crowd and realized she would have to turn some people away.

"Just the muffin and a cup of coffee, right?" She handed her a brown bag and tipped her head at the coffee urn on the table. "I got that brown sugar you wanted, Ms. Ryder."

Three other women inched closer to the tall, reed thin, gray eyed woman.

"We are with her."

Clearly, they were latching on to her. Philomena Ryder didn't look very pleased. With a slight shrug of her bony shoulders, she took the muffin and stepped toward the coffee.

Jenny began handing out the rest of the food. She had placed a small carboard box beside her to gather cash, trusting people to pay her the right amount. Captain Charlie lingered, sipping his coffee, staring at the big ship anchored in the distance.

"Did you get a bite to eat last night?" Jenny asked him. "You must've run dozens of trips in your boat."

One of the local girls had been hired on as part of the service staff. She had packed something for him.

"I was full." He patted his stomach. "Chunks of steak and lobster, some cheese I couldn't recognize and those Old Bay wings you made. But no cannolis."

Jenny promised she would make a batch for him. Some of the locals had told her the same and she surmised the kitchen had run out.

"You better make those wings too. I think they should be on the new menu."

The Old Bay wings were a recipe she had been tinkering with, considering how the islanders loved the spice and herb mix that got its name from the Chesapeake.

"Were they too hot?"

His response was drowned out by a shrill scream that startled all of them. There was no doubt it was a woman. Before she could figure out the direction, Captain Charlie had slammed his coffee cup on the table and was off at a run. Jenny prepared to follow him.

"Where you off to?" the next man in line demanded. "I want my breakfast."

"But ..." Jenny stared back, wide eyed.

"Probably one of them rich ladies from the big boat, having a lark."

Jenny hoped he was right. She began dispensing the rest of the food, barely looking up until she heard a woman say the word Sheriff. Her head jerked up. Two squad cars had arrived at the boardwalk, their lights flashing. She saw Adam Hopkins marching across the beach, headed for the pier.

"What's he doing here?" someone voiced.

Jenny was wondering the same. She handed out the last two muffins and put a hand painted sign saying 'Sold out' on the table. There was a collective groan but the crowd began to disperse. Feeling her energy drain, Jenny sat on a chair and looked around for her phone. Whatever was going on at the pier, Betty Sue would have heard of it.

Heather bounded up the steps, pulling the leash attached to her poodle Tootsie. Impatient as always, she picked up the little ball of fur, slightly out of breath.

"What a night, huh." She gushed, full of praise. "I've never had so much champagne. Billy saw the label and said it cost two hundred bucks a bottle. Is that so?"

"Billy knows his wine."

Jenny scanned the beach for any activity while Heather rambled on, recollecting the fancy dishes she had eaten for the first time.

"The Lombardis know how to throw a party. I think the town was wrong about them. They didn't have to invite the lot of us, right? Dario is a generous man."

"What are those cars doing here?" Jenny asked.

Heather looked surprised. She hadn't noticed the police presence on the beach.

"One of the old biddies at work, I bet. Some trivial complaint."

Jenny shook her head. Adam would have come back by now if there were no issues.

"I'm going to see for myself."

Heather gave a deep yawn and waved her off.

"Tootsie and I are going back to the inn for a nap."

Jenny started walking on the boardwalk. She could see a few people huddled together near the pier. Adam stood with his feet planted apart, flanked by two deputies. The crowd was trying to peek over their heads and the cops were holding them off, asking them to stay back.

A woman sat on a bench nearby with a blanket around her shoulders. One of the female deputies stood by her. Whatever had made the woman scream, Jenny was certain it was not trivial.

She broke into a run, panting as she got closer. Then she veered to the side, heading close to the waves, assuming it would give her a clear view of what Adam and his men were shielding. Her guess was right. Nobody noticed her inch toward them. A loud gasp escaped her, drawing Adam's attention.

A body was sprawled in the sand and it wasn't moving. Jenny didn't have to be told the man was dead. The first thing she noticed was the dark hair, parted in the middle. Her eyes widened in horror as she made the connection.

"Oh no no ..."

Adam appeared in her line of sight and turned her around.

"You shouldn't be here, Jenny."

"Wait a minute, Adam. Tell me what happened to him. Did he drown?"

He took her arm and forced her to walk away.

"I can't say anything right now. Mostly because I don't know myself. But this is a crime scene."

Jenny stopped and stared into his eyes.

"Are you sure? Maybe he's just drunk and sleeping it off."

Adam wasn't listening.

"Did you check his pulse, Adam? Why haven't you called an ambulance? We need a doctor here."

He told her the medical examiner was on his way. It took a few moments for his words to sink in.

"Dario Lombardi is dead!"

Jenny's eyes filled up. She had solved many murders since she came to Pelican Cove but had rarely encountered a dead body herself. And it wasn't a stranger. It was a man she had interacted with several times in the past few days. Dario Lombardi was a loud, arrogant and insensitive lout. But Jenny had believed he had a benevolent side.

"Will you please go back home?" Adam pleaded. "I promise to call you once we wrap this up."

Jenny gave in.

"He liked my cannolis. The chocolate was his favorite, studded with salted pistachios."

Chapter 4

Jenny couldn't get the image of Dario's dead body out of her mind. At least she hadn't got a look at his face. The Magnolias twittered around her, talking about something inconsequential. They were trying to divert her without much success.

"This coffee is good," Betty Sue held up her cup. "But it could be so much better if it was brewed here."

"The foreman says he'll be done in a few days."

"And hasn't he said that a dozen times before?" Star huffed. "I think you're too good to them."

Molly agreed, telling Jenny she needed to put her foot down.

"Escalate this." Heather suggested. "Let's go to the Cohen Constructions office and give them what for. They must provide a firm date now."

Her friends weren't entirely wrong, Jenny realized. The renovation that was supposed to take a week at the most had stretched on over two months. But she trusted her contractor.

"The workmen are not idle. In fact, they do overtime on most days."

Didn't that cost her more money, Betty Sue wondered.

"What I mean is, it's just a matter of days. The café will reopen and you can get your fresh coffee."

Heather argued that she could set up a coffee machine on the deck. The others struck down the idea at once.

"There's too much dust in the air." Molly sneezed. "We're good with what we have, Jenny."

Star turned toward her niece, a look of concern in her eyes. "Do you want to talk about it, sweetie?"

Jenny shook her head. She hadn't really known Dario Lombardi. Though not quite a stranger, the man wasn't her friend.

"He told Billy last night was the greatest of his life. The Isabella was his dream project and it was going to make him loads of money."

Maybe one of his business rivals had got rid of him, Molly mused.

Jenny gave a shrug. There was no need to assume Dario's death was anything but an accident. He had gone overboard with the drinks and landed in the water somehow.

"I say it's one of his family," Star declared. "Did you see how menacing they all look?"

That got a laugh out of Jenny. She knew her aunt was just being facetious.

"He might have made some enemies in the past. I guess they came looking for him."

Molly pointed out the Lombardis were a crime family. Nothing about them was usual or predictable.

"There's a lot of money involved here," Heather added. "Like millions. What does Adam say, Jenny?"

He hadn't told her a thing. But Jenny hoped he would share some details with her once he found out more.

"There's that boy himself ..." Betty Sue pointed at the boardwalk.

Sure enough, Adam sauntered toward the café. He gave a wave when he caught all the Magnolias looking in his direction.

Jenny got up to fix him a cup of coffee, handing it over when he came up the steps.

"What have I done to deserve this special treatment?" he teased. "You ladies look like a tiger waiting to pounce on his prey."

"I don't have any cookies or muffins to go with that," Jenny said. "And I'm not even sure if the coffee is hot enough."

Adam sat down between Star and Heather and took a long sip.

"It's better than what I'll get at the station so I'm not complaining." He peered at the roof and pointed his cup toward the kitchen. "How's the work going? I hear the natives are getting impatient."

Jenny gave a shrug. She had stopped agonizing over it.

"Don't give her a hard time," Betty Sue admonished. "The poor girl's been running around town, delivering meals. You think she doesn't want the work to be done?"

Heather interrupted her grandmother.

"Enough of this small talk. Give us the real scoop, Adam."

He flashed her a grin, well versed with her impatience.

"The body on the beach is indeed Dario Lombardi. You ladies must have already heard that but it's official now."

"Yeah, tell us something we don't know." Star quipped. "Did the fool drown himself or did he have help?"

Were they dealing with murder, Jenny probed.

"Too early to say anything. We are focusing on how he got there and when. It's going to take a lot of old fashioned police work to establish these timelines."

He would not say more. Jenny recognized the hard set of his mouth and chose not to pepper him with any more questions. Adam left and the group dispersed, Jenny and Star heading home to make lunch.

"You're running ragged, sweetie." Star spoke as she diced celery for chicken salad. "I hate this."

Jenny began packing the stack of pimento cheese sandwiches she had prepared. She had come up with the idea of a limited menu for lunch for those who depended on the café for their midday meal. Her customers welcomed the kind gesture and were thankful.

"What would I do otherwise? I'm not one to sit on the couch and flip channels on television. At least not anymore."

Jenny's earlier life as a suburban mom had been one of luxury. She couldn't help marvel at how much she'd changed.

"Do you miss it?" Star guessed what she was thinking.

"Not really. I mean, it gave me Nick. And I was happy. Billy was a good husband, until he wasn't." She began scooping chicken salad on thick slices of wheat bread. "But my life's great now too. I have no complaints, Aunt. My cup runneth over."

Jenny sorted the sandwiches according to the orders and placed them in large cloth bags. Star would take one back to the Boardwalk Café. Jenny drove around town to deliver the others.

They had a quick bite at the kitchen counter before they left. The phone rang just as Jenny slung her handbag over her shoulder.

"Unhunh ... unhunh ... I can guess what that means. Okay, we'll be there, of course."

Star had guessed the caller.

"What does she want?"

Jenny told her Betty Sue had called an urgent town meeting that night. She wanted to strike while the iron was hot.

"Why do I feel this has to do with the Lombardis?"

The afternoon passed quickly. Jenny did some prep in the kitchen after she was done with the deliveries. She put her feet up for a while and read a book. Then it was time to get ready for the town meeting. Jason was in the city and was not going to make it. Star called to say she was already at the Bayview Inn with Betty Sue.

The sun was setting as Jenny drove into town. The Isabella was silhouetted against a gray sky mottled with pink and mauve. Unlike the previous day, hardly any of her lights were on. The ship looked like a ghost. Jenny brushed off the thought, telling herself she was being fanciful.

People streamed into the town hall, taking any seat they could find. There was a buzz of anticipation. Everyone was curious about the agenda and expected something delicious that would provide them with free entertainment and a topic of conversation for the next few days.

Betty Sue sat on the raised platform, with Ada Newbury and a couple of other geriatrics. Barb Norton, a statuesque woman who spearheaded most of the town events, stood at the podium, pulling at the string of pearls around her neck.

Jenny walked to the second row and slid in beside Molly. Billy sat on her other side.

"Hey Jenny!" He raised his eyebrows. "Ready for a good show?"

The meeting was called to order and Barb Norton began. As Jenny guessed, the town committee wanted the Isabella gone from their shores.

"A gruesome murder took place today," Barb spluttered. "Or last night." She darted a glance at Adam and frowned. "The Sheriff won't give us any details. But I say the citizens of Pelican Cove have a right to know."

A few people clapped and others chorused their assent.

Barb ceded the stage to Betty Sue.

"We have tried to get rid of this casino before. We didn't succeed. But the murder changes everything. Who knows what went down last night?"

The crowd took that as an open ended question. Eddie Cotton from the Rusty Anchor was sure it was a drug deal gone bad. Williams from the grocery store said it was revenge.

"Gangster business." He stood up and rove his hand around the room. "Just like in the movies."

There were some sniggers and Williams sat down, gratified.

An old fisherman told them they were all wrong.

"It's the old curse. Nothing good can come of naming that ship Isabella. We warned those goons, didn't we? Now look what happened. That fine young man is dead for no reason."

The younger members of the audience laughed at him, saying he was being ridiculous.

Betty Sue pounded the gavel, ordering them to shut up.

"We have prepared a petition that is being circulated around the room right now. I want everyone to sign it. The Lombardis will have to leave when they see the whole town is against them."

Ada Newbury stood up and walked to the podium. She had to elbow Betty Sue away.

"You can take as many signatures as you like. These people are not going anywhere."

Chapter 5

Jenny stared at the column of figures before her at the Boardwalk Café the next day. She couldn't make the numbers add up. She looked up and stared at the water, forcing herself to take deep breaths, trying to tamp down the panic that rose in her throat. The café renovation had exceeded the original budget several times. She was going to need every penny she had saved to finish the project.

A bank of clouds moved in, obscuring the sun. Thunderstorms were expected later that afternoon. The atmosphere was heavy and Jenny had been dragging her feet since morning. At least all the breakfast customers had come and collected their food. One of the women had cribbed at the lack of variety. It had taken effort to ignore her.

Jenny began gathering all the papers strewn on the table, giving herself a stern talk. Out of nowhere, a wave of anxiety rolled over her and she felt the hair on her arms stand up. There was a thud on the steps and Jenny looked up, surprised to see a strange man come up on the deck.

He was fairly tall and stocky, with light brown eyes that didn't hold any hint of emotion. Her eyebrows shot up when he came up to her table and sat down. She stifled the urge to look around. The foreman was inside with three men and there was a man on the roof, doing something with the shingles. But she was alone on the deck. If she hollered, one of them would surely come running to her aid.

A corner of his lip went up and a smirk settled on his face. Jenny felt he had read her mind and was laughing at her.

"Quinn." He introduced himself. "I'm a private investigator."

"Quinn what?" Jenny burst out. "Is that a first name or a last name?"

"You don't need to worry about that."

The family had hired him to look into Dario's death.

"You mean the Lombardis?" Jenny confirmed. "Why?"

"None other. You need to respect them if you value your life. People like them do what they want. They do not entertain questions about their actions."

Jenny refused to be intimidated by him. She folded her arms and stared back, her mouth set in a firm line.

"You don't think they are gonna wait for the police to make an arrest? They want me to apprehend the killer before the police so they can deal with him in their own way."

There was no point in asking him to elaborate. Jenny hoped she was able to hide her disgust. She wanted the man gone from her deck.

"Why are you here?"

Quinn looked around him, taking his time to answer.

"Isn't this a café? What does a man have to do to get a cup of coffee here?"

"We are closed for renovation."

Quinn put a leg up on the table and placed his arms above his head.

"I talked to the locals. It seems you like getting beat up by murderers." He gave a dry laugh. "Why don't you join forces with me?"

It was the last thing Jenny had expected from him.

"I go for the truth. What if the Lombardis are involved in Dario's murder? I've heard enough about them to know it's not a stretch."

Quinn told her that was impossible. The family had invested big money in the Isabella venture. It was Dario's baby and they needed him to make it profitable. There was no doubt the ship and casino would make all of them a lot of money.

"People on the island worship you. They are more likely to open up to you."

"We have a perfectly good police force, Quinn. I have a lot on my plate now so I don't think I want to be involved."

His eyes bore into hers, cold and sinister.

"I'll be in touch."

He was up in a flash and walked off, leaving Jenny gaping after him.

A part of her wasn't pleased that he was ordering her about, taking her for granted. She owed him nothing. But did she owe Dario Lombardi? Whatever his past, he had given her an opportunity when she needed it. And he had made her feel special, allowing her to showcase her talent before a string of celebrities who would otherwise never set foot in the Boardwalk Café.

She was curious too, of course. Solving murders had become second nature and the casino owner's death was a puzzle she wanted to put together. But what if she did manage to figure out the mystery? There could be consequences she had no control over. As Quinn had mentioned, who knew how the Lombardis would react? She didn't want to be an instrument in the hands of the family. What if they killed the person she pointed to? She would be aiding and abetting in another murder.

Jenny grew agitated at the churn of thoughts in her head. She contemplated going for a walk. A glance at her watch told her it was time for the Magnolias to arrive for coffee. Sure enough, Heather came up the steps, brandishing a thermos. Jenny had run out of coffee that morning and requested

Heather get some from the inn. Betty Sue huffed up the steps, accompanied by Star. Molly was close behind.

"We got news." Star declared.

Jenny had forgotten all about the meeting the two older ladies had been in that morning. She gave her aunt an encouraging smile.

"The spring festival will start next week, right on schedule." Betty Sue declared. "And it's going to be a disaster!"

Heather had been fixing coffee to everyone's liking. She handed out the mugs and Molly passed them around. There were some oatmeal raisin cookies to go along with it.

"Why do you say that, Grandma?" Heather picked up her mug with both hands and took a sip. "Barb Norton ruffle your feathers again?"

Star defended Betty Sue. Ada Newbury and Barb Norton had gone behind the festival committee's backs.

"They are bringing in outsiders!" Betty Sue blurted. "This has never happened in the history of Pelican Cove."

"You say that about a lot of things," Heather quipped. "Isn't it time we did something new? What we do today is going to belong in the town's history tomorrow."

That was why it was necessary to follow traditions, Betty Sue insisted, not change them. It was a sore point with her. She predicted all kinds of dire scenarios.

"We are already dealing with one murder. Didn't I say nothing good would come from the Isabella? Now these out of town food trucks Ada is promoting are going to create more problems for us."

Molly asked Jenny if she was making cannolis, trying to steer the conversation to neutral ground.

"I have to." Jenny waved at the papers before her. "Let's hope the food trucks bring in more business. It's going to take me years to pay off this renovation."

Star mentioned the time and Molly stood up, ready to go back to the library. Jenny needed to go home herself to start preparing lunch.

For the second time that morning, a stranger arrived on the deck of the Boardwalk Café.

He was short and bald, with a large belly hanging over his low slung khakis. There was a big black mole on his nose, giving him a clownish appearance. Jenny thought the man was very unfortunate in the looks department. She stared at the chunky gold chain around his neck. Two buttons of his shirt were open, revealing a hairy chest.

"Antonio Bellini." He gave a slight bow. "But everyone calls me Tony. And let me guess." His dark eyes traveled across the group, lingering on Heather before moving on to nod at Molly who held a pile of books in her arms. "Molly, the librarian."

He pointed at each of them in turn and guessed their names correctly. Jenny couldn't hold back any longer.

"I'm sorry, Tony. Who are you and how do you know us?"

He laughed. Unlike the investigator Quinn, Tony sounded friendly.

"I'm Leona's cousin."

Jenny's eyes grew wide as she connected the dots. Leona! He meant Petunia, of course. Not a day went by when the Magnolias didn't talk of her. She had passed in an unfortunate accident a few years ago.

Petunia owned and ran the Boardwalk Café when Jenny first came to Pelican Cove. She had given Jenny a new purpose when she had no idea what to do with her life. After she passed, they learned she had been living under a false identity. Her real name was Leona and she was the daughter of Enzo Bellini, a powerful mafia boss.

One by one, the Magnolias had realized who the man was. Tony had their undivided attention.

"Are you here because of the casino?" Betty Sue made a shrewd guess.

"That's right." He agreed readily.

Jenny didn't remember seeing him at the party on the Isabella.

"The Lombardis are our business rivals," he laughed again. "Dario sent me an invitation but the old man would not have approved. So I stayed away."

Which old man was he referring to, Lombardi or Bellini?

Jenny apologized for not having anything to offer him. They had eaten the cookies Molly brought and drunk all the coffee.

"No worries, no worries." He replied smoothly. "Look, I won't lie to you. I was sent out here to scope the area. Dario wasn't the only one who thought of setting up a casino here, you know. Thanks to Leona, we know how beautiful this place is. And it's isolated, not on anyone's radar, if you get my drift."

That would make it easy to conduct any nefarious activities, Jenny guessed. The Lombardis must have thought the same.

Tony appeared to be in good spirits, easily accepting his mission had been a failure. He wanted to visit Petunia, since he was in town.

"I'm glad I met you all. Can one of you lead me to her? I would like to pay my respects."

Betty Sue appeared mollified. She nodded at Heather who wrote down the directions on a napkin. Tony glanced over it and thanked her.

"So long then." He looked around. "You're taking care of the old place, I see. Let me know if you need any help. Err, Uncle Enzo is rolling in the dough, you know. He'll gladly chip in."

Jenny hoped her thoughts weren't transparent. They all said goodbye and watched him go down the boardwalk.

Heather slapped her hand on the table.

"That is the real shocker of the day!"

"What's he really doing here?" Jenny burst out. "I mean, why are these people suddenly interested in our town?"

Molly thought the outlook was dire. Somehow, the town had caught the attention of these powerful families. Who knows what activities they planned to conduct there, away from the hawk eyes of the big law enforcement agencies.

"Forget the food trucks, Betty Sue," she warned. "Think of how to get rid of the Lombardis."

Heather offered the parting shot.

"You don't want Pelican Cove to become a hub for criminals, do you Grandma?"

Chapter 6

Jenny sat on the patio in her garden, dressed in an oversized soft sweater and jeans. She sipped from a glass of wine, listening to Jason talk about his day. They rarely got an opportunity to sit like this and she cherished the moment.

"This is really good wine." She praised, knowing Jason took pleasure in picking out selective wines for her.

Jason gave a broad smile and brought up the café.

"We should throw a party when we reopen."

With a shrug, Jenny told him she was ready to do whatever he wanted as long as she got the café back in her hands.

"The customers are getting antsy. And like them, I'm also tired of eating the same sandwich for lunch every day."

Jason laughed out loud. That's what she got for spoiling them.

"They are used to pancakes and fancy omelets for breakfast and gourmet meals for lunch. Of course they don't want the humble chicken sandwich."

Talking about the café had reminded Jenny of the accounts she had been going over that morning. A frown settled between her brows. Jason picked up on her consternation immediately.

"What's the matter, honey? Don't keep anything from me."

He listened patiently while she laid out all the extra expenses they had incurred. Then he gave a low whistle.

"We are not just off budget. I think this is an entirely new project, one we never planned on."

Did he think the Cohens were ripping her off? Jason struck down the idea immediately. They had a reputation for being fair and diligent, plus they worshipped Jenny.

"They will never forget what you did for them, when you solved that murder. If you ask me, they are probably doing it at cost."

Jenny accepted she had never considered that. She needed to go to the construction company's office and have an open conversation with them. There was no need for them to give her any special consideration.

The sun plunged below the horizon while they were talking and they went in to eat. It was getting too chilly outside.

Jason set the table while Jenny pulled out a pan of baked fish and roasted vegetables and heated the sauce to make a teriyaki glaze.

"What's going on with Nick?"

"He's just finishing a big case. Maybe we'll see him for a whole weekend soon. Billy's excited."

Jason was fond of Jenny's son. They had a lot of common things to talk about, being lawyers.

"Nick's an intelligent young man. I have no doubt he'll make partner in that firm in record time. But what about his life outside the office?"

Jenny speared a piece of salmon and dipped it in some sauce. Darting Jason a frustrated look, she took a bite and began to eat.

"You're asking me this? Nicky's so focused on his career, he doesn't have a spare thought for anything else in his life. Billy was the same and I'm sure you were too."

Jason gave a slow nod.

"I was. I had crazy hours until I made partner at my old firm in the city. One fine day, I woke up and realized I was thirty five."

That's when he had chucked his high flying job and come back to Pelican Cove, opting for the slower life.

"What about love, Jenny?" He extended his hand and placed it over hers. "I spent half my life without the love of a good woman. But I missed out."

Jenny ate the last chunk of potato on her plate and grimaced.

"That's what I want for him, Jason. I want my boy to fall in love with a good woman. He needs to realize what the real blessings in life are. Not a fancy car or a fat bank account, although they don't hurt. But a partner who will stand by you no matter what."

They both agreed to broach the subject with Nick when he came home. Jenny had never taken on the role of a matchmaking mama but she was ready now.

They moved to the living room and Jason watched a game while Jenny rifled through a lifestyle magazine.

"No dessert?" Jason gave a yawn.

Jenny offered ice cream with homemade fudge. The clock in the kitchen told her it was getting late so she only fixed one bowl.

"Don't forget your coat." Jason watched her pull on her sneakers. "And come back soon."

He patted the spot next to him on the couch. The lights were dim and the fire added a cozy warmth, casting shadows across the room. Jenny gave a low groan but stuck to her resolve.

It was a cold night and she put her hands in the pocket of her coat, taking deep breaths of the refreshing salty air. A few steps later, she picked up her pace. She had become used to these solitary walks. It was a time to reflect on her day, even her life. The beach was almost private and the only other person who came there was Adam.

A furry yellow Labrador came bounding up to her, his tongue hanging out. His eyes were full of joy as he climbed up to her chest and gave her an enthusiastic lick.

"Hello sweetheart!" Jenny fondled him lovingly, pulling out a ball from her pocket.

She threw it wide and the dog gave a woof and ran to fetch it.

"You spoil him." Adam walked up to her. "Hi Jenny!"

He looked preoccupied.

"Are you tense about this case?"

"You have to stay out of this business, Jenny." Adam was serious. "I mean it. This is not a reflection of your abilities. We all know you're a good sleuth and very capable of solving any murder. But this is different."

"Because of the Lombardis?" Jenny guessed.

They were dangerous, Adam stressed. Who knew what resources they had and the lengths they would go to. Old man Lombardi was not happy about losing his son. Dario had been the youngest and a favorite with the head of the family.

Jenny had wanted to tell Adam about Quinn, the investigator who had visited the café. But some instinct told her to hold back. Unable to resist finding out more, she asked if there were any new developments.

They walked a few paces and stopped. Adam turned around to face her.

"Dario was strangled. That much is evident. But we have not been able to determine the time of death. It's because he was dumped in the cold water. That makes it hard to determine, simply put."

So there was no doubt it was murder, Jenny mused.

"Best estimate now is around midnight," Adam continued. "We are checking all the camera footage and the exits. Also parts of the ball room or the areas where most of the guests were."

There had been fireworks. A majority of the guests had been engrossed in the show. Had someone taken the opportunity, hoping to go unnoticed? That did not explain how Dario's body had ended up at the pier. What did Adam say about that?

He rubbed his temples, sighing in frustration.

"I have nothing. As I said, Jenny, we are just beginning to look into things. Tracing his movements that night is imperative. Most of my staff is engaged in doing that."

Jenny realized he had said nothing about suspects. Did he believe one of the locals was responsible?

"Are you going to interview us? Most of the locals were present on the ship that night."

Adam didn't give her a direct answer. According to him, Dario's death was just inconvenient. The man had a sketchy past. There was no secret he came from a criminal background.

He must have more enemies than they could count on the fingers of their hands.

"Any of the guests could have had it in for him? Or for the family. They wanted to target one of the Lombardis."

Jenny realized he made sense. Maybe this kind of a thing was very common in the world the Lombardis lived in. Betty Sue's strong objection to the casino made sense now. The Isabella had brought violence to the shores of Pelican Cove. That was exactly why the town council and some of the older people had protested so strongly. Could one of them have taken matters in their hands?

Adam laughed out loud when she voiced what she was thinking.

"What! Do you think the welcome wagon did it? Took him a platter of cookies and strangled him?" He chuckled. "I didn't expect this from you, Jenny."

Two big splotches of red appeared on Jenny's cheeks and she blushed furiously.

"Surely it's not that farfetched? You heard what some of them said at the town meeting. One old man talked of shooting at the Isabella with his rifle."

"Yeah, sure." Adam needled. "And the ghost of one of the sailors from the sunk Isabella rose from the ocean and used a rope to strangle poor Dario."

That was the last straw. Bristling with indignation, Jenny whirled around and stomped away.

"Wait!" Adam came after her. "Jenny, please. I didn't mean to offend you."

Refusing to give in, Jenny set a rapid pace for home.

Her mind whirled with various scenarios. Adam was right, of course. There had been several guests on the ship. The Lombardis must know at least some of them for years. Who knew what scrapes Dario had got into in his life? He might have duped innocents, robbed poor families or misbehaved with someone's daughter or sister. He must have hurt someone badly enough to make them want to kill him.

Adam was right. This was a job for the police. They could conduct background checks and had the manpower to interrogate dozens of guests. On second thought, she agreed with him. Dario had been murdered by someone from his past. That eliminated anyone from Pelican Cove. She gave an involuntary laugh, trying to picture Barb Norton going on a rampage to kill Dario.

Her mind moved on to the next question. Had the murder been planned in cold blood, or was it a spur of the moment act? One of Dario's enemies must have cornered him on the ship and taken the opportunity to get rid of him.

Chapter 7

Jenny took a pan of muffins out of the oven the next morning and set them aside to cool. Then she made two big batches of scrambled eggs and began packing the food. Star hadn't been in the house when Jenny woke up. She assumed she had gone out on the bluffs to paint the rising sun.

Tidying up in the kitchen, Jenny set off and delivered the food to her elderly customers. This was a different routine than what she had become used to over the past few years. She enjoyed being out and about in the early hours, getting some fresh air. It was so different than being cooped up in the café kitchen for most of the morning. The renovation would change things a lot. Jenny looked forward to the slightly enlarged space and the big window they had put in over the kitchen sink. It would let in light and air and also give her a good view of the beach.

People had already lined up on the deck and boardwalk by the time she reached the café. All the breakfast bags were dispensed in the next fifteen minutes, except one. The coffee was gone too, much to her chagrin. She had been craving a cup. She glanced at the one remaining bag. It belonged to Philomena Ryder. She was a woman with a hearty appetite who often ordered two muffins along with eggs. And she was generally at the front of the line. Jenny wondered what was keeping her.

Unable to sit still, Jenny hopped down to the boardwalk and took a small walk. She stayed within sight of the deck, in case anyone appeared and needed her.

Half an hour passed. There was no sign of Philomena. Beginning to feel concerned, Jenny decided to call. She telephoned the woman, waiting for her to answer. Three attempts and several rings later, it was clear Philomena was either not at home or was not coming to the phone. That's when Jenny made up her mind to visit.

A quick call to Betty Sue gave her the information she wanted. Philomena lived just a few blocks away. Jenny confirmed the address and picked up the bag containing her breakfast. She set off at a fast clip. Ten minutes later, she stood before a charming Cape Cod with daffodils blooming in the garden.

The doorbell produced no response. Trying to tamp down an irrational fear, Jenny walked around to the back. She climbed up two short steps to a screen door and banged on it. Was that a faint cry? Jenny rattled the handle and realized the door was not locked. She pushed it open and rushed in.

"Ms. Ryder?" she called. "Philomena?"

The cry was stronger this time. Jenny followed the sound to what was a spacious bedroom. Philomena lay on her back, a duvet rumpled at her feet, a pained expression on her face.

"What's wrong?" Jenny placed a hand on her forehead. "I am sorry to barge in like this but I was worried." "I'm Jenny King," she added. "From the Boardwalk Café."

"Of course I know who you are," Philomena smiled. "Will you help me sit up, please?"

Jenny assisted her, managing to prop her up against a bank of pillows.

"Bless you, child. I wondered what was going to happen to me."

Jenny thought the situation was not very dire. One of the lady's friends or neighbors would have gone looking for her. Philomena managed to refute that.

"All three of my friends – neighbors – are out of town. One's in Japan on vacation, another's visiting her kids ..." She sighed. "It's my back, you see. I must have pulled something. There's a spasm when I try to move."

They needed a doctor. Jenny proposed calling an ambulance. Philomena was looking at the bag at Jenny's feet.

"Is that my breakfast? You'll think me a glutton but I am starving. Do you mind if I eat something first?"

"Oh, oh, of course!" Jenny realized her gaffe. "How remiss of me. Let me get some coffee started. Or do you prefer tea?"

Philomena was a committed coffee drinker. She directed Jenny to the kitchen. There was a bag of premium Colombian roast, to her delight. Soon, the kitchen was redolent with the strong, enticing aroma of a medium roast coffee while Jenny heated the food in a microwave. She plated the food, arranged everything on a tray and took it back to Philomena.

"I put cream and sugar in." She handed a cup to the woman. "And I found this in the refrigerator." She held up an ice pack. "This will ease some of the pain." Jenny placed the tray on her lap.

Philomena thanked her again and began eating with gusto.

"I drink this coffee every day but it's never as good." She smiled. "You have the magic touch, Jenny."

"It's just coffee."

"I hope you have eaten?"

Jenny realized she had barely grabbed a bite herself. Her expression must have revealed that because Philomena offered her half a muffin.

"Nothing doing. No point in starving yourself."

Jenny looked around the room. It was spacious, with a bank of windows along one wall. A deep, luxurious Persian carpet surrounded the king sized sleigh bed. There were shelves in two corners, overflowing with books. A large flat screen TV was hung on the wall in front of the bed.

"As you can see, I spend a lot of time in this room. So I've filled it with things I love. Nothing beats watching reruns of old Hollywood movies, snuggled in my bed."

Jenny agreed with her, getting caught up in Philomena's story. She was a retired county clerk and had never married. There had been a beau but he went to Vietnam and never came back.

"I spent forty five years at that job. It didn't pay a lot but I was frugal enough to set aside a nest egg. Now I plan to live the rest of my life in the lap of luxury. The house is paid off, I'm healthy and all set to start hitting my bucket list."

She was a descendant of one of the survivors of the Isabella.

"Unlike the others, I'm not superstitious," Philomena muttered. "So I didn't care what they called the ship. And I didn't mind going to that party either. Hey, I'm not going to say no to a fancy dinner I don't have to pay for.

But this murder ... I object to murder."

Jenny let her talk.

"The ship needs to leave right away. I hope Betty Sue Morse is doing something about it." Philomena ate the last bite of her eggs. "That's imperative if we want the spring festival to succeed. All the tourists who come to town will go to that ship."

The Isabella was a threat to the local businesses. But it was not going to be easy to ask them to leave. The town had no authority over the Lombardis. Even if the town council dug up some law they were breaking, the family was too powerful.

"Harry Campbell already came to blows with them." Philomena continued. "If I hadn't known him since he was a snotty kid, I might have wondered if he killed that funny man."

Jenny sat up in her chair. This was news to her. She offered to refresh Philomena's coffee. A quick trip to the kitchen and a steaming cup later, she wondered how she might ask for details. But there was no need. Philomena turned out to be quite garrulous.

"That man promised to hire the Steakhouse for providing food on the ship. Harry ordered supplies. He must have spent a lot on them, he was that angry. I'm sorry dear, but he was mad because they chose you instead."

Jenny told her it was fine. She was planning to square things with Harry.

"Harry Campbell ranted at him. Said his business was in the red because the locals thought the Steakhouse wasn't good enough. Not only had he lost on the new business, but his old customers were also deserting him. He blamed that pudgy man for his downfall."

Jenny's impromptu mission of mercy had produced some unexpected information. Philomena admitted she was feeling drowsy. She had spent a sleepless night. She permitted Jenny to call her doctor. A visit was scheduled. Feeling she had helped as much as she could, Jenny took her leave.

The sun had risen in the sky and she rallied in its warmth on her walk back to the café. She spied her friends on the deck and picked up her pace, hoping someone had brought snacks.

There was a plate of coffee cake on the table. Betty Sue had baked it that morning. Jenny served herself some and ate a bite.

"This is delicious!" she exclaimed, full of praise. "When are you giving me the recipe?"

Betty Sue's hands were busy knitting something lavender. "You know when."

Star wanted to know where she had been. Why hadn't she left a note or sent a message to someone?

Jenny told them about Philomena.

"That one loves her food." Betty Sue grumbled. "I hope you haven't promised her lunch. She'll make you run ragged."

"I don't mind. The poor woman has no one."

Heather asked what she thought about the food trucks staying in town for the length of the festival.

"See, earlier we assumed they would go back to wherever they came from. But they want to camp here now. It's got the old biddies in a tizzy."

She glanced at her grandmother.

"What's the harm in letting them stay, Grandma?"

Jenny told her to rewind a bit. The last she heard, the town committee was against allowing outsiders at the festival.

Betty Sue had bowed before overwhelming pressure. She could not use her veto every time, so she had given in.

"They do have some interesting food on offer. One of them is setting up a smoker for pork ribs. I'm partial to some."

There was a vegan truck, one with gourmet sandwiches, a falafel stand and an Indian restaurant from Newport. All of them had food the locals were not offering. Betty Sue had made sure of that.

"It will be very hard for them to drive back and forth every day, considering they will be working ten to twelve hours. Why not let them stay?"

Betty Sue pointed out the hurdles. They would need hookups for water and the use of some facilities. Ada Newbury had suggested they allow the food truck owners to use the High School's gym for the purpose.

Jenny could see how the old guard would see it as an encroachment.

"Well, I'm off to see Harry Campbell. I need to clear the air with him, make sure he doesn't hold me responsible for this supposed ruin of his."

She wanted to question him about his fight with Dario. She needed more details than Philomena had offered.

"I can guess your real purpose, Jenny." Molly stood up. "You better not confront him alone."

Like Philomena, Betty Sue had known Harry Campbell since he was a baby.

"That's funny!" she chortled. "Are you saying Jenny should be afraid of him?"

Chapter 8

"Don't you have to go back to work?" Jenny asked Molly on the way to the Steakhouse. "I'm not afraid of Harry. We have gone there often enough in the past few years."

Both Jason and Billy chose the Steakhouse when they wanted a good steak. Jenny herself loved the food there. It had the familiar comfort of the recipes she grew up eating. Nothing fancy, just good old hearty American food.

Molly was serious.

"Harry was a good friend of my father's. He's like an honorary uncle. So yes, I believe he's harmless. Actually, I have never seen him in a bad temper. That's why I was surprised to hear he was in a full blown argument with Dario Lombardi. That is completely unlike him."

Molly thought she could pacify him if he became fractious.

They arrived at the Steakhouse. The front door was closed since the restaurant only opened for dinner. But Jenny knew her way in.

They entered via a side door and followed the sound of voices to the dimly lit dining room. Harry sat at a table below a chandelier, dressed in his uniform of khaki shorts and a floral shirt over a white vest. There was a line of sweat on his brow and the table before him was strewn with a pile of receipts. A short, bespectacled man Jenny had never seen before stood before him, his head bowed.

"Blast it!" Harry exclaimed. "This is not enough, man. We're going under."

He glanced up when Jenny cleared her throat. His eyebrows shot up and his eyes turned red.

"You! Come to gloat at my misfortune?"

Jenny let out an involuntary gasp. The bitterness in his tone cut her to the core. Harry Campbell had never spoken to her like that.

"Hello Uncle Harry." Molly came forward.

His mouth tilted at the corner and he opened his arms wide. She walked into them and embraced him tightly.

"Been a long time since we went fishing, munchkin."

Jenny stood by while they exchanged some pleasantries. How had Molly never mentioned her connection to Harry? She tried to get a word in after some time but Harry ignored her.

"Please Harry. Can we talk?"

His gaze hardened again as he turned toward her. He waved his arm around, pointing at the table.

"Can't you see I'm busy? No time to shoot the breeze. Not all of us have steady business from the casino, eh? Some have to sweat and toil to earn their daily bread."

Jenny asked when she could return. Would an hour later suit him?

"I was trying to be nice." Harry bit his lip. "But the answer to that question is never. Not on your life. You are not welcome here, Jenny King!"

That did it. Her patience at an end, Jenny lambasted him.

"Did you talk to Dario Lombardi on the night of the party?"

Harry's eyes flickered. Jenny was almost sure he would not answer. Then he surprised her by giving a slight shrug.

"I had a mind to stay away, especially after that dirty trick they pulled on me. But why should I miss a good party? Did I not spend a bundle trying to cater for it?"

Captain Charlie had convinced him to put in an appearance. There was no point in burning any bridges.

"He took me to the Isabella. I was there for a short time. Shook some hands, spoke to a few people before I left. That's it."

Harry flipped through some receipts as he said this. Jenny realized he wouldn't look her in the eye. The man was lying.

"So you didn't meet Dario?"

"Didn't I just say that?"

"I know you are lying, Harry. What I don't understand is why."

Harry bristled with anger.

"What gives you the right to give me the third degree like this, missy? The man is dead. Any business he might have thrown my way is gone." He slammed the bunch of receipts on the table. "You have done all the damage you could. Whaddaya want now?"

Molly patted the man on his shoulder and urged him to calm down.

"Just get her away from here," Harry fumed.

Molly took Jenny's arm and pulled her away. Reluctant to anger the man further, Jenny followed her out of the restaurant.

"The nerve of that man! He lied to me outright."

Molly seemed puzzled. She defended Harry Campbell. She had known the man all her life. He was known to be fair and straightforward. He sponsored kids from less fortunate families, making sure they finished high school. Any man out of a job could depend on Harry for some part time work at the Steakhouse.

"Uncle Harry is one of the most honest people I know."

Jenny was sure he was hiding something. Molly offered an alternate theory.

"How do we know Philomena Ryder is right? She didn't actually see him, did she? She just thought she heard his voice."

"That's true. You think she was mistaken?"

Molly thought it was possible, although she couldn't say for sure. There were many people on the ship and Dario had business dealings with a lot of them. He might have been arguing with any of them.

On a whim, Jenny whirled around and went back inside, ignoring Molly's protests.

"Just tell me one thing, Harry." She barged in. "What time did you leave the Isabella that night?"

"I don't need to respond to that. Now spare me the trouble of having you thrown out."

Harry's answer would not have made much of a difference. They did not know exactly when Dario died or where. Jenny backtracked and tried to pacify Harry.

"Please don't be upset. I'm trying to figure out a few things for Dario's sister."

Harry's eyes bulged and he guffawed, shaking his head from side to side.

"That's rich. If you are playing detective again, Jenny, that woman is the one you should be looking at. Dario and big sis were sworn enemies."

"What?" Jenny tried to hide her excitement. This was news to her. "Thank you, Harry. No hard feelings."

She beat a retreat without waiting for his response.

Molly was nowhere to be seen. Jenny guessed she had gone back to the library and began walking to the café. She was already running late. Star accompanied her back to her home Seaview and the two made sandwiches in record time.

"I'm exhausted." Star climbed up on a stool at the kitchen counter. "Would you mind if I stay back, sweetie?"

Jenny glanced at her aunt and noticed the circles under her eyes. Star was painting a large mural at the Boardwalk Café, depicting all the scenic spots around the island. She had been working long hours, trying to finish the job before the café reopened.

"Do you promise you'll take a nice long nap after lunch?"

Jenny drove back to the café, wincing at the people waiting for her. She apologized profusely and began handing out the bags.

"How much longer before the café opens?" one lady grumbled. "It might be spring but the weather's chilly enough for soup."

Jenny made some promises once again, wondering the same. She craved a big bowl of chicken noodle soup herself. There were two brown bags left over after the last customer left. Jenny tore one open and began eating a pimento cheese sandwich. She was hungry.

"Any more of that?" A familiar voice hailed her.

Captain Charlie climbed up the steps to the deck. Jenny greeted him with a smile and pointed at the remaining bag.

"You're in luck. I packed two bags for us but Star stayed home. It's chicken salad."

They decided to split the two sandwiches between them so they could have half of each. Captain Charlie finished his half in three bites.

"What are you up to, Jenny? Got that new menu finalized?"

He must have been to the Steakhouse. Captain Charlie had an ongoing deal with his friend Harry. The restaurant had first dibs on his fresh catch. In return, he could eat there any time he wanted.

"Harry Campbell is a good man."

Jenny assured him she had nothing against Harry. She had just wanted to ask him a few questions, based on what Philomena Ryder said.

"Not the easiest of women."

"Really? She was very nice to me."

"That's because she needed you," Captain Charlie argued. "Never done anyone a favor."

He asked why Jenny was getting involved in the murder. The stakes were different this time.

"No telling what those folks might do. Let the police handle it."

"Adam said the same."

Captain Charlie wolfed down the last bit of sandwich and spread his hands wide.

"Well then. Why borrow trouble? It's not like any of us knew that boy."

He was referring to Dario, of course.

Jenny brought up her visit to the Steakhouse. Harry had been very harsh with her.

"He's always been so friendly. I didn't see that coming."

Captain Charlie was quiet.

"I should never have made those cannolis."

She had not realized her cooking would have such a negative impact on a local business. Jason had taken her on special dates at the Steakhouse. She had fond memories of the place.

"You don't really think it will shut down?"

Captain Charlie told her Harry Campbell had hit a rough patch. Hopefully, business would pick up once tourist season started. If not, the town would pitch in to help. Jenny realized he was being modest. He would bail his friend out if needed.

"This is a rough time for him. Both of his sons were killed in action on the front. It was three years apart but it happened in March."

Jenny had not known that. Did he not have any other family? Captain Charlie told her his sons' widows had opted to live in the city with their kids. Neither of them was from Pelican Cove. The grandkids visited in the summer.

"I'm glad you told me that. Maybe I'll make him a care package. What kind of cookies does he like?"

Captain Charlie's eyes twinkled.

"Chocolate chip. And he's partial to pine scented candles. Just make sure you don't make any cannolis."

Jenny gave a snort, asking him if he was sure. Her cannolis had become the talk of the town.

"Harry's a standup guy, Jenny. He would never lie to you."

Chapter 9

Jenny went home, yearning to put her feet up. The whole episode with Harry Campbell had left her miserable. Star had left a note for her on the kitchen counter. There was a bowl of soup in the microwave, along with strict instructions to stop blaming herself.

She knows me too well, Jenny sighed. Heating the soup took a minute. She found a hunk of sourdough bread in the refrigerator and dipped it in the warm broth, trying to calm her thoughts as she chewed. Just when she was thinking longingly of taking off on a vacation, the phone rang. It was Molly.

"We're having a spa night."

"Tonight?"

"Yes, Jenny. I think we all need a break."

Why hadn't she thought of that? Jenny gave her wholehearted approval and reminded Molly to get the brownies.

"Do I ever come without them?"

The rest of the afternoon was spent in prepping for the next day's meals. Finally, Jenny trudged upstairs for a bath. She reveled in the lavender scented bubbles and sat back in the tub in pure bliss, her mind empty of thought.

Star was bustling in the kitchen when she got ready and went down.

"Chamomile tea." Star handed her a cup. "I used that wild honey from the farmers' market in Exton."

"This should get us in the mood." Jenny took a bracing sip.

The sun had begun its downward journey when the ladies began to arrive. Heather came first with Betty Sue, with a shopping bag.

"Got some bright nail colors. They are perfect for spring."

Molly arrived, holding a large Tupperware box they knew well. Jenny broke tradition and opened it right away, picking up a brownie. She took a big bite.

"Sorry Molls. But I need chocolate. It's been that kind of day."

Heather cut her off. They were not going to talk about anything stressful.

"No talk of murders or festivals or town related stuff."

She gave Betty Sue a stern look. "Am I clear?"

They all agreed readily. The next two hours were spent in blissful pursuits like manicures and pedicures, face masks and giving each other foot massages. Heather was painting Jenny's toes in a shimmering coral shade when Jason arrived.

"Hello everyone! I had no idea this was a spa night."

He promised to leave for the Rusty Anchor after a quick shower. The doorbell rang again. Heather rushed to the door, cash in hand, and flung it open.

"Pizza!" she cried. "And Billy."

They had ordered three large pies with big salads. Billy sauntered in, planting a kiss on Heather's forehead.

"You never told me you were having a spa night, honey." He grumbled.

Heather explained it was impromptu. She suggested he go to the Rusty Anchor with Jason. He was just coming down from the stairs. The air was full of the hearty aromas of Mama Rosa's pizza sauce. Jason begged for a slice.

"I'm so hungry," he told Jenny.

Betty Sue declared there was plenty of pizza for everyone. The men could stay, as long as they remained out of sight. They agreed readily and disappeared into the kitchen.

The evening wound to a close after the food was gone. Jenny's mood had improved a lot and she felt ready to take on the world. Star had retreated to her bedroom and the others were back home.

"Shall we go for a walk?" Jason offered her his arm. "Or are you too tired?"

"I'd be delighted."

They pulled on their coats and stepped out into a moonlit night. Jenny wove her arm through Jason's, resting her head on his shoulder. Neither of them said a word, content in being close to the other.

Jenny spotted a lone figure in the distance, throwing a stick in the air. Tank leapt after it. He came running to Jason, holding the stick in his mouth. Jason realized he wanted to play.

Adam greeted them. Jenny poured out her suspicions about Harry Campbell.

"Harry? Come on, Jenny. Philomena Ryder is not very reliable."

He told her they were evaluating a number of people and would not spare anyone. If Harry was guilty, he wouldn't escape.

Jenny had to be satisfied with that. Loathe to let go of the sense of wellbeing the spa night had produced in her, she didn't ask any more questions. She was yawning her head off by the time they reached home.

A sound eight hours produced the desired results. Jenny was bursting with energy as she prepared breakfast the next morning. A vague plan was forming in her head. She finished all her deliveries, saving Philomena for the last.

"Are you feeling better?" she asked the older woman.

"The doctor came and wrote me a prescription. He wants me to rest for a week. I start physical therapy after that."

Jenny took her leave, eager to reach the café and serve her other customers. Captain Charlie was there. He sat at a table, digging into his eggs.

"Do you have any charters today?" Jenny asked. "If you're free, can I hitch a ride to the Isabella?"

He put his fork down, staring at her in dismay.

"Did you forget something on the ship? I can ask one of the kids to look around and get it the next time they come ashore."

Jenny shook her head. She wanted to meet the Lombardi family. Especially Dario's sister.

"Have you met her?" She didn't mention what Harry had said about her.

Captain Charlie told her he knew her well. She would not give Jenny the time of day.

"That's the way she is with everyone. Hoity toity, if you know what I mean."

Jenny pressed her lips together, unwilling to give up.

"No harm in trying."

She told him about the private investigator. He had seemed shady. At the very least, Jenny wanted to confirm if he was really working for the Lombardis.

It was a dreary day with an overcast sky and a chilly wind. There was no sign of spring. Jenny bundled up at Captain Charlie's behest, wrapping a wool scarf around her neck. They set off in his boat and soon, Jenny was climbing aboard on a lower deck. A security guard stood by the elevators. He asked why she was there.

"I have a meeting with Ms. Lombardi." Jenny blustered.

The guard wanted to know if she had an appointment. Jenny told him she had some important information about Dario to share with the family. The guard stepped aside, but Jenny saw him speak into a walkie as the doors closed.

She rode up to the main floor where the party had been held. It was the heart of the ship, a kind of atrium. The place was deserted. There was no sign of any guests. What had happened to all the people who attended the party?

"You have news about Dario?" A sultry voice demanded.

Jenny found herself face to face with a tall, voluptuous woman with fleshy lips painted a dark red. Every feature of her body appeared magnified. It was probably because of the tight dress she wore, revealing a large expanse of bosom. It was obvious that she had invested in a lot of cosmetic surgery, some of it unfortunate. Her large eagle shaped nose was flattened on one side, making her look grotesque.

"Ms. Lombardi?"

"Yeah, yeah. I'm Bianca Lombardi. Whaddaya want?"

Jenny introduced herself. Dario had hired her to curate the party menu.

"You're the cook from that tiny island?" She spat. "I have no idea why Dario brought you on board when we have the best Michelin starred chefs working for us."

"It was a privilege. Your brother was very kind to me."

Bianca started shouting orders, sending the staff scurrying to follow them. Jenny wondered if she had forgotten her presence.

"Why are you still here?" Bianca jabbed a finger at her. "You don't expect me to give you a ride ashore?"

"No, no." Jenny cut to the chase. "Do you know a man called Quinn? He came to see me, claiming he was working for you."

Bianca's lip curled in a sneer when she heard the name.

"Him? So what?"

"Is he looking into Dario's death? Who do you think is responsible? Did he have any enemies?"

Bianca laughed. Jenny felt a shiver pass through her.

"Dario liked to play the genial host. That's what he was doing, inviting all those rustic people from the island. But his real job was different." Her eyes bore into Jenny's. "You know that, don't you? You've heard of the family?"

Unable to come up with a suitable response, Jenny could only nod.

"Of course Dario had enemies! People who woulda' loved to get even with him. What kinda fool question is that?"

Jenny was taken aback. Bianca's behavior was rough, to say the least. She rushed ahead with her next question before she lost all courage.

"Were any of them on board the Isabella that night? At the party?"

With a shrug, Bianca walked to a nook decorated with a couple of plush couches. She raised her hand and a young waiter appeared, carrying a martini on a tray.

"It better be a double." She barked before taking a long sip. "Big and dirty, that's how I like 'em."

She demanded to know why Jenny was grilling her.

"Quinn came to ask for my help. I need to know a few things before I can do anything."

Bianca's face broke into a smile. The martini was gone and a second one had been placed in her hand.

"You're that old woman who digs up bodies." She cackled. "Quinn said he was going to butter you up because you have an in with the Sheriff."

Jenny let the comment slide over her.

"You must have talked to Dario that night?"

"Sure, a couple of times."

Did she remember the last time? Bianca paused, then told her it was some time before midnight.

"Before that big toast Papa made. Now that you mention it, Dario wasn't with us."

Had he gone missing before that, Jenny wondered. Maybe Dario was already dead before the big celebratory toast.

"Did you go looking for him?"

Bianca slammed her glass down on a side table.

"Are you an imbecile? I just said I had no idea he wasn't present at the toast."

Jenny ignored the insult. That seemed to annoy Bianca.

"Papa gave the toast and we mingled with the guests. Primo and I. But there was no sign of the kid."

Wasn't that odd, Jenny probed.

"He had this habit of disappearing in the middle of things." Bianca tapped the side of her nose. "Important stuff. So we didn't think it was a big deal."

But someone had clearly hurt him. If she had to guess, who would she pick.

"Dario had a reputation for being mean. Nobody dared cross paths with him. Whoever killed him must be really powerful. Even more so than the Lombardis."

Jenny pressed her for a name, sure she was holding back. Her persistence paid off. Bianca swore under her breath and spread her hands wide.

"Senator Worth. He has power and money. Loads of it. He was screaming at Dario earlier that evening, demanding his cut from the casino."

Chapter 10

Jenny was quiet on the ride back to the shore. The sky was darker than before and a storm was forecast for later that afternoon. A few drops of rain fell and Captain Charlie opened the throttle, trying to get back before they were drenched.

"What's on your mind, dearie?" He scratched a spot on his cheek. "These rich people have a mind of their own. I wouldn't pay too much attention."

"Are you talking about Bianca?"

Captain Charlie nodded. The woman didn't have a kind bone in her body. She often abused the staff, promising dire consequences if they didn't do her bidding.

Why did they work for her then, Jenny asked, feeling naïve. Captain Charlie gave a shrug. Needs must.

"I took her measure in seconds." Jenny said. "So I ignored all the slurs she sent my way. I can be thick skinned when needed."

"Then what's brought on that frown between your brows, missy?"

Jenny debated talking about the senator. The Lombardis were menacing enough. She didn't want the wrath of a powerful, possibly shady politician to rain on Pelican Cove. Least of all, a sweet man like Captain Charlie.

She told him she had chosen to take his advice. The police would handle the murder. There was a lot of work before her and she wanted to start planning the grand reopening of the café.

"And the spring festival's almost here. I better start producing all those desserts everyone expects."

They reached the dock and Captain Charlie gave her a hand. He secured the boat and walked beside her to the parking lot where her car was.

"I've never known you to back off like this. Are you that afraid?"

"You can't have it both ways!" Jenny shot back.

Captain Charlie laughed. He wondered what she was keeping from him.

"You remember I was in the Navy? I have seen some action in my time, fought in wars." He paused, took her arm and turned her around to face him. He placed his hands on her shoulders.

"Whatever's frightened you, I can take it. Just let it all out, Missy. No point working yourself in a tizzy."

Jenny expelled the breath she had been holding and told him about the senator.

"Did you hear that? A crooked politician. As if having a crime family set up camp in our town is not bad enough."

Captain Charlie was quiet. Then he asked what she really wanted to do. Did she want to go and question the senator?

"You think he won't entertain you? Or are you saying he'll hurt you in some way?"

Jenny shook her head. She was at a loss. Part of her did not believe Bianca. She looked like a woman who sought attention. Maybe she was just being sensational by pointing to the senator. On the other hand, why would she choose him out of all the other guests on the ship? No doubt, the Lombardi family was getting some favors from Senator Worth. If she had a sound business sense, she would not endanger their relationship.

"He has a lot of power at his disposal," she added. "If Bianca is right, and the senator did murder Dario Lombardi, I'm small fry."

They reached her car. Captain Charlie opened the door and shut it after she slid into the driver's seat.

"Aren't you putting the horse before the cart? We don't even have a motive. If the Senator wanted to get rid of that punk, he might have done it in a dozen legal ways. There was no need to send him to the other world."

Jenny smiled. Captain Charlie was right. If Dario had committed plenty of crimes, there must be many cases pending against him. If the Senator was aware of the nefarious activities the Lombardis carried out, he might use his connections to get one of them arrested.

"You're a wise man. Am I seeing you for lunch?"

She promised to save a sandwich for him and drove off, realizing she needed a quick trip to the grocery store. The next hour passed in making and packing lunch. She finished her deliveries, looking in on Philomena Ryder again.

"Hello there!" she beamed. "I'm sitting up in bed."

The doctor was pleased with her progress.

"I'll be fine just in time for the spring festival. Ooooh, I heard about those food trucks and I can't wait to sample everything."

Jenny agreed the outsiders would provide some much needed variety.

"You will make those cannolis though?"

"Yes, I'm working on a couple of recipes with strawberries and chocolate."

Back at the café, Jenny dispensed all the brown bags. She had a brief powwow with the foreman who gave her the same spiel as usual. They were almost done.

Jenny wanted to peep in the kitchen but he had cordoned off the area.

"No, no. Mr. Cohen said you must wait for the big reveal. You're going to be happy with what we did, Ms. Jenny. I promise!"

Jenny entered the main dining area. At least Star was allowing her to see the half done mural.

"You've done a lot this week," she praised. "This whole wall is stunning! The tourists are going to go crazy taking pictures with that backdrop."

It had been Heather's idea, wholeheartedly approved by Mandy, their marketing consultant.

Star cleaned her brushes, admitting she could use a break. They went back to the deck and ate the sandwiches. Jenny produced a brownie she had saved from spa night.

"Chocolate does make everything better," Star sighed.

They talked about the cannoli recipe Jenny was trying out. She was planning to use a strawberry ricotta filling. Then she would dip the whole thing in melted chocolate.

"Can't wait to taste it, sweetie. And now I better get back inside."

Jenny ran a damp cloth over the table and sat there, thinking about her trip to the Isabella. She had obtained new information but wasn't sure she could act on it.

The wind had turned fierce. Grains of sand flew in the air, making it hard to see in the distance. Jenny didn't notice Adam coming down the boardwalk until he came up to the deck.

"Hi Jenny!"

She was surprised. Had he forgotten the café was closed?

"You don't expect me to feed you?"

He gave her a sheepish grin.

"I needed some air. I guess I came here by habit." He ran a hand through his hair. "You know what? I completely forgot the café is closed."

Jenny sensed he was preoccupied.

"Is it the Lombardis?"

They had no break in the case, Adam lamented. The forensic team was still working on the meagre evidence they had found, trying to come up with something tangible. It looked like Dario's murder would remain unsolved.

"Are you sticking to your promise?"

Jenny told him about her brief ride to the ship. Adam frowned but let her continue her story.

"The grand restaurant, the casino, the Isabella itself, it was all Dario's project. He bragged about how it was going to be his most profitable venture yet."

Adam just gave a shrug. The man was a big talker. He had been trying to woo the locals. That didn't mean he was right.

"That's not what I'm saying. The Isabella and that party was important to Dario. I think I heard someone complain about inviting all the locals. But Dario had insisted, it seems."

There was no way Dario would miss the big toast at midnight, unless there were extenuating circumstances.

"You mean he was dead."

Adam told her the police had also tried hard to trace the man's movements. He had disappeared just before midnight.

"Have you questioned all the staff then?" Jenny was curious. "Are they willing to talk to you?"

The local staff Dario had hired was very forthcoming. They expected to be fired any moment. And they would remain in town after the Isabella was gone. But the crew on deck was another story. None of them were cooperative.

"Most of them must be loyal to the Lombardis," Jenny reasoned. "But Dario was also a Lombardi, right?"

Adam shook his head. The crew was terrified. An old sailor who worked in the engine room had revealed that silence was a part of their job description. They had all been warned. Nobody wanted to test the bosses and see what happened if they said something.

"But withholding evidence is a crime," Jenny offered.

The police could not accuse everyone on board of doing that. All they could rely on was technical evidence. Adam and his staff were going through all the camera footage. It was a laborious task.

"We were hoping to figure out where the victim was before he died."

Jenny leaned forward, eager to know what they had found. Adam shook his head.

"No luck, Jenny. All the camera footage for an hour around midnight is missing. Wiped out."

"On purpose?"

Adam stood up and began pacing the deck. He stopped suddenly, staring at the roiling ocean, his hands on his hips.

"I believe so. Someone covered their tracks, very deliberately deleting anything that might have helped our investigation."

Chapter 11

Jenny spent the afternoon making cannolis. There was no one to taste them so she summoned the troops. Heather and Molly arrived together.

"There's another town meeting tonight." Heather announced. "We need to wind all this up in an hour. Can't be late."

Molly loved the spicy note the strawberry and cheese filling had. She thought the chocolate overpowered the taste of the berries.

"What if I dip just one end in the chocolate?"

They tried both options and came up with a winner. Then it was time to leave.

Jenny went up to wash and change her outfit. They generally ordered pizza from Mama Rosa's after the meeting and came home to Seaview to rehash what had gone down. But spa night had just happened. Maybe Jason would have something else in mind.

The thunderstorm had passed through town and left clear skies in its wake. The ground was still wet though and the air was cold. Jenny yearned for warmer weather and knew it would be there soon. That would bring the tourists and she hoped the café would be open by then.

She rode to the town hall with Heather. Jason was going to meet her there.

"What's the agenda for today's meeting?" she asked.

Heather told her it was all about the spring festival.

"They are fighting over the spaces. Now that the food trucks from out of town are being allowed, the locals are demanding first dibs on all the prime spots."

Betty Sue was pounding the gavel, ordering the crowd to settle down when they reached. She glared at them, mouthing that they were late.

Harry Campbell was all fired up.

"First that ship, now this. Are you bent on ruining us, Betty Sue? You want the Survivors eliminated, is that it?"

Mr. Williams from the grocery store began protesting. Eddie Cotton from the Rusty Anchor pub joined him.

"The Pioneers have always supported your lot," Mr. Williams roared. "You wouldn't be here otherwise."

One of the young bucks who had recently moved to town demanded to know what nonsense they were talking about. He was a millionaire who had earned a lot of money by shorting some stock during the subprime mortgage crisis of 2008. Now he was spending his days working out in his home gym, developing an energy bar that would be the next big thing. He had opted for a booth to sell high protein food. Naturally, he expected his opinion to be heard.

"Why don't we focus on the real issue here?"

Mr. Williams got worked up. The real issue was that the Isabella was a blight on Pelican Cove. It had always been that way.

"You don't know the history of this island. It was called Morse Isle first. Betty Sue's ancestor bought it for a few hundred dollars. He moved here from up north and built a house for his family. Then he invited his special friends to settle here. People like the Williams and Cotton families with impeccable bloodlines."

"And the Newburys," Ada interrupted from the stage. "The Newburys were here before you, Harry."

Eddie Cotton joined the milieu. They blamed the survivors of the Isabella for increasing the population of the island, making it dangerous to live.

"Big chunks of land fell off in the ocean in the Great Storm of 1962," he told to whoever would listen. "My grandpa always maintained it was because of over population. Those survivors grew like wild grass."

Harry Campbell pumped a fist in the air.

"That's right. The Survivors have always outnumbered the Pioneers. You're almost extinct." He pointed at Heather. "That one's never having kids. So the Morse bloodline is gone. Same for the Newburys. That boy never married again. And what about your boy Chris?" He dissolved into laughter. "No, no. You have to listen to me, Betty Sue. I say we assign all the main spots to our own people."

Jenny had a stitch in her side from trying not to laugh. She and Heather pinched each other, trying to keep straight faces. The meeting stretched for an hour.

A woman Jenny had never seen before accused the town council of taking kickbacks.

"Pelican Cove has become a hotbed of corruption. My poor Daddy's turning in his grave." She clucked, shaking her head from side to side. "For shame, Betty Sue, how could you let this happen?"

"What are you saying?" Betty Sue boomed.

The woman accused her of taking money from the food truck owners. Everyone knew the Bayview Inn was deserted in the off season. This is how Betty Sue was filling her pockets.

That ended the meeting. Betty Sue came down from the stage with Adam's help and walked out. Heather, Jenny and the other Magnolias followed. Ada and Barb Norton joined in. Soon, the whole hall was empty, except for the three or four people who were still arguing at the top of their voices.

"I need a good meal." Betty Sue declared, summoning Billy with a crooked finger. "Normally I would have gone for a steak but I'm not taking any more of that Harry Campbell. Take me to the Crab Shack."

They all piled into their cars and headed out. Ethan Hopkins welcomed them with a grin.

"Harry's loss is my gain. That was some meeting, huh?"

Jenny hadn't noticed him in the town hall.

"You were there?"

"I couldn't get away but news travels fast. Adam will be here to vent, no doubt."

They occupied a large table close to the water. Most of the food on offer was fried, which seemed perfect for the cold night. The servers brought trays of onion rings, mozzarella sticks and coconut shrimp with a variety of dipping sauces.

"Do you think Ada is preferring certain people over the others?" Star asked Betty Sue.

"She's always played favorites. But she's not doing it for money."

Everyone knew the Newburys had plenty. Jason and Billy both started talking about the latest movie. Jenny took the cue and broached the topic they had been wondering about.

"When are you getting married?" she asked Heather. "Our wedding planning will have to begin according to that."

Heather looked at Billy. He answered with a shrug.

"We're not sure we want a big fuss."

It was Billy's third wedding. They all knew that. But Heather was going to be married for the first time.

"You better not be thinking of eloping." Betty Sue warned.

Star stroked her friend's back, trying to get her to calm down. Jenny thought she had hit the nail on the head. It was just the kind of thing Heather would find attractive.

She gave the couple a stern look.

"Whatever you do, make sure we are a part of it. Your family? We want to be there to wish you well and shower you with our blessings. And Nicky will not want to miss it either."

Ethan arrived with more fish. There were pan seared fillets of cod, with mango salsa and a honey chipotle sauce. He was trying out a healthier menu for the summer.

"Can I trust you to be honest? Tourists want lean options these days. My chef's learning to use a pan."

A series of objections traveled along the table. They came to the Crab Shack when they were craving fried food. Was he going to change the entire menu? Ethan assured them the classic dishes would still be on offer.

Jenny was more flexible than the others. She loved the fish and thought the salsa could use a kick.

"A little more jalapeno pepper," she told him. "Most islanders like spicy food so it shouldn't be a problem."

Ethan tipped his head toward the bar. Adam sat there, nursing a beer. He looked exhausted.

"My brother said the same."

Seeing Adam reminded Jenny she hadn't been upfront with him. What if he came to know later that she had withheld information? She didn't want to lose his trust. So she excused herself from the table and walked over.

"Hey!" she began. "That was some meeting."

"Gets crazier every time," he grumbled and glanced at their table. "Lemme guess. Betty Sue couldn't take any more of Harry."

They both laughed. Jenny decided it was now or never and rushed ahead.

"Can we talk? There is something I have to confess."

He picked up an onion ring from the plate before him and dunked it in the creamy dip. An enigmatic smile appeared.

"I guessed as much. You're not that inscrutable, Jenny."

What he didn't say was he knew her too well. She started telling him about the Senator. Adam listened without interrupting her, lapsing into thought when she asked if it was possible to interview him.

"He's a busy man. I'm sure he'll claim he can't leave the city. So we'll have to go to him."

Did he mean she could tag along?

"You might disarm him. He's more likely to open up. But we'll have to be very careful about what we say. No point in getting sued for libel, or whatever injustice he'll claim."

Why did Jenny think he might have murdered Dario? She wasn't sure about the motive. But Bianca had seen him argue with her brother. It was a matter of covering all their bases. Maybe Senator Worth would give them a clue that would lead them to the real killer.

Adam proposed leaving the next morning.

"Bright and early, okay? How about we start at seven? It will take us two or three hours to reach Washington D.C."

Jenny's first thought was the café. She would have to recruit someone else.

"Eight's better for me, or seven thirty. I'll have to finish the breakfast deliveries at the very least."

Adam agreed with her. Jenny went back to her table. Jason was settling the check and the others were curious.

"Out with it," Heather prompted.

Her face stretched into a smile the moment she heard about the drive to the city.

"Road trip!" she chortled. "It's gonna be fun."

"I don't think Adam will ..." Jenny began to protest.

Betty Sue cut her off.

"We're all going!"

"But what about breakfast? And lunch?" Jenny protested. "I was going to beg you all to pitch in while I'm gone."

Star suggested a solution. They would accomplish the deliveries, slightly earlier than usual. Jenny could provide the lunch sandwiches at the same time. That would take care of her seniors. The rest could take a day off from the café.

"You need a break, sweetie. And it's not like you're gonna engage in fun and frolic. There's a cold blooded killer out there. The sooner he's behind bars, the safer it will be for everyone in Pelican Cove."

Jenny set her alarm for earlier than usual when she reached home. She slept soundly and woke up with a purpose. Star was already pottering around in the kitchen and the smell of freshly brewed coffee filled the air.

They worked in tandem, assembled all the bags and Jenny went up for a quick shower before setting out for the deliveries.

"Be careful," Jason warned. "I'm a good lawyer but I may not be able to save you from the might of a Senator."

The Magnolias were waiting in the driveway when Adam arrived. He gave a groan when he realized they meant to accompany him.

"This is ridiculous!"

"Don't be a jerk, Adam Hopkins." Betty Sue thundered and climbed up into the passenger seat of his SUV. "You can drop us off at the mall. We won't be cramping your style."

Jason had a meeting in the city too so Jenny drove with him until they reached the big mall at Tysons Corner. She gave him a quick peck and promised to be circumspect. Then she joined Adam in his car.

"Are you ready for this?" She glanced sideways, trying to gauge if he was tense. "I hope you are not feeling intimidated."

He gave a dry laugh.

"Come on, Jenny. I'm a soldier first and foremost. And let's not forget, this man is the people's representative. He works for us!"

Chapter 12

Jenny was a bit apprehensive about going to meet Senator Worth. Would he have an office in the Capitol? She had been to the Mall area several times, of course, but always as a tourist. When her son was younger, she had taken him to the Smithsonian, the Air and Space Museum, even the Spy Museum. They visited the monuments each year for the cherry blossoms. But she had never actually been inside the power center.

"Suddenly, I'm not so sure about this," she muttered, drawing a smile from Adam. "Why are we going to Georgetown?"

They had taken the exit and Adam slowed as he entered the city street. His deputy had called the Senator's office for an appointment. He had agreed to meet them at his home.

"He has an office there too, I guess," Adam shrugged. "It's more private. I think he wants to avoid any gossip. It's good for us, Jenny. He will be relaxed and maybe his guard will be down."

Jenny noted Adam wasn't wearing his Sheriff's uniform. But even in a formal blue shirt and khakis, he still exuded authority.

They inched along the quaint cobblestone streets, stopping frequently for pedestrians. Georgetown was one of the most expensive suburbs of Washington D.C. Billy had talked about buying a house there. But that had been just before they broke up.

"Does he live in government provided quarters?" Jenny inquired.

Adam shook his head. His research had revealed that the Worths were an old and respected Boston family who had produced a long line of war heroes, governors and politicians.

"He's a third generation Senator. The family has served several Presidents." He braked at a stop sign. "They all have an impeccable record."

Jenny was impressed but she refused to be intimidated. She had seen the Senator aboard the Isabella. So there was no doubt he hobnobbed with the Lombardis. Surely he had something to gain from them?

Adam thought politics as a whole was a gray area. Ultimately, anyone standing for office needed funds for their campaign. And they were not very circumspect about where that money came from.

"You mean he's taking money from them."

"He could be!"

The GPS announced that they had reached their destination. Tall iron gates guarded a rambling three story structure made of red brick. Adam waved his credentials in a camera and drove through when the gates swung open.

A girl in her twenties waited outside to show them in. She was dressed in a smart dark suit, with a figure hugging skirt that ended well above her knees. Her energy made Jenny feel very old.

"The Senator has a very busy morning," she proclaimed. "He has managed to set aside fifteen minutes for you, against my advice."

She halted mid step and gave them a warning look.

"Stay on topic. No small talk. The sooner you're done, the better it is for the country."

Jenny stifled a laugh.

The girl provided some details about the property. It was two hundred years old and had been bought by the Worth family just after the second World War ended. All the Senators lived there when the house was in session.

There was nothing informal about the office they were shown into. It was a massive room, furnished in dark tones. A thick carpet covered the floor. The furniture was all made of leather in a rich brown hue. Jenny recognized one or two of the art pieces on the wall and tried not to gape.

The Senator sat behind a massive mahogany desk, all smiles. He didn't get up.

"Good morning!" he greeted affably, his blue eyes the color of a summer sky. "I hope you had a pleasant journey."

No wonder he got elected term after term, Jenny thought. It was impossible to not be charmed by his manner.

"You must be Sheriff Hopkins." He shook hands with Adam. "And who is your companion?" His eyes bore into Jenny's.

She tried not to squirm under his steady gaze.

"Just my secretary," Adam lied smoothly. "She's here to take notes."

Purely out of instinct, Jenny trod on his foot, making him cry out. The Senator didn't miss a beat, flashing a smile at her.

"As long as you're not a reporter." He leaned back in his chair. "My press secretary will read me the riot act if I talk to one of you without being prepped."

The girl who had ushered them in sat on a sofa placed by a wall. The Senator gave her a slight nod. She sprang up and left the room.

"We are here to talk about Dario Lombardi," Adam began. "Do you accept you knew the man?"

The Senator nodded, encouraging him to move on.

Adam asked how he knew Dario. How long had he known him? The Senator gave generic replies without actually revealing anything. Then Adam brought up the day of the party.

"Can you tell us when you went aboard?"

The Senator had arrived just before lunch. He went into a lot of detail about how he had travelled. A charter plane had brought him from Washington to Norfolk. The Lombardis had sent a limousine to pick him up. He had to share it with a young pop singer. They were taken to the Isabella by one of the ship's tenders. He was shown to his stateroom.

"It was more luxurious than expected," he told them. "Dario had an eye for detail. He always wanted to be an interior decorator. Can you imagine? A man of that background helping you choose upholstery?" He laughed at his own joke.

There had been a lavish lunch followed by a siesta. That was code for getting some work done in his cabin.

"I never have an off day," he complained. "There is always some policy to draft, letters from constituents, sponsors to reach out to."

Jenny was not feeling sympathetic. Clearly, the man was putting up a smokescreen. She caught Adam's eye. He was deadpan.

"When did you leave the Isabella, Sir?" he asked. "Can you give us a general idea?"

"After that midnight toast and the fireworks. Great show. I hope you didn't miss it."

Jenny agreed it had been spectacular. Had he waited to have supper after that?

"No, actually. I had an early meeting here the next day. My driver was waiting at the wharf and we drove through the night and came straight home."

Adam got down to business. Had he talked to Dario that day? The Senator seemed incredulous.

"But of course! He was the host, wasn't he? Dario was there to welcome me aboard that morning. We had lunch together. Then I saw him at the party. He was circulating through the crowd then so we didn't talk much at that time."

Adam thanked him for being so cooperative.

"Where were you after 11:30 PM? It will be great if we can establish your movements between then and the time you left the ship."

The Senator's smile didn't falter but Jenny saw his eyes flicker for a fraction of a second.

"That's a tough one. I was busy talking to so many people. That party was a politician's dream, you know. All those small town, salt of the earth type people in one place. They may not be my constituents but it was a great opportunity to further the party's agenda. The leadership appreciates this kind of spontaneous action."

Once again, he was trying to misdirect them, Jenny thought. Adam was silent, waiting for the man to talk himself out. The tactic worked.

"Look!" The Senator exclaimed suddenly, his composure slipping a bit. "I know where this is going. You're trying to pin a murder on me. Not gonna happen, Sheriff. First of all, you don't have a motive. Dario Lombardi was just an acquaintance. To be honest, I wasn't very keen on attending that party. But it's been very busy here these past few months. It was a hall pass, if you will. A chance to grab some quality time alone and mooch on expensive food."

He confessed he was a gourmand. Dario Lombardi knew that. One of the Michelin starred chefs had been lured to the Isabella, just to entice the Senator to attend.

"My presence increased his cred with the old man."

Adam switched tracks. Did the Senator suspect anyone? Who would murder Dario Lombardi?

"The Bellinis, of course." Senator Worth quipped. "I hear Tony Bellini was in town that day. See, I don't know if you're aware of all their history. The Bellini and Lombardi families have a vendetta against each other. In fact, this whole casino on a ship that anchored offshore was Tony Bellini's brainchild. He thought they could shift their location every few weeks, making the most of every location. Somehow, don't ask me how, the Lombardis got wind of the idea. Dario beat him to it."

He paused to take a breath.

"Tony must have lost face with his family. He contacted my office many times. Wanted my help to set the whole thing up."

Adam latched on to that. Had the Senator assisted Dario then? What made him choose the Lombardis over the Bellinis?

The Senator had recovered his equilibrium. He glanced at his watch, appearing impatient.

"I didn't have to. They followed the application process and it went through the usual channels. My staff had nothing to do with it."

The door opened and the girl from earlier stepped in.

"Sir, your next appointment is here."

He stood up this time, fastening the button of his suit jacket. It was the end of the interview.

"Keep up the good work." He flashed another mega watt smile. "Let me know if you need any assistance."

The girl was ushering them out before they finished giving their thanks. They were out of the house and on the steps outside in record time. Adam's car was right before them, engine running. A man in a valet's uniform was holding the door open.

Jenny held her breath until they exited the iron gates.

"Whew!" Adam expelled, running a hand through his hair. "I hope I don't have to do that again."

"He turned on the charm for us."

"I think it must be second nature to people like him. There's always a camera around, ready to capture their unguarded moments."

Adam parked on the street after a couple of blocks.

"I need coffee," he pleaded. "And maybe a pastry of some kind."

They crossed the street, reading the signs on the stores. Jenny spotted a café she vaguely remembered from her previous life. Adam ordered lattes and assorted pastries and suggested going to the waterfront.

"We can sit on a bench and recharge our batteries."

Jenny liked the idea. It was barely noon. She called Heather to see what the others were doing. They made plans to meet for lunch.

An hour later, they were sitting down in an Italian restaurant, eating big plates of pasta and risotto served homestyle. Adam had ordered the osso bucco.

"Is this what we pay you for?" Betty Sue teased. "You better not mention a word of this to your cronies, Adam. Or you'll find yourself the subject of the next town meeting."

There were shouts of laughter at that. Jenny was glad to see Betty Sue cracking jokes. The trip had softened her mood which was good. They needed to take more trips so she could distance herself from the town issues.

"What did the Senator say?" Heather quizzed. "Do you think he's guilty?"

Adam was noncommittal but Jenny didn't hold back.

"I can't say if he was the one to kill Dario but I sensed one thing. He's not entirely innocent."

Chapter 13

Jenny wanted to buy something for Jason so they spent an hour at the mall, trying to find the perfect leather wallet. His old one was frayed and he had complained about it once or twice. She came across a silk tie she couldn't resist. Then Heather had to get one for Billy.

They finally set off and merged onto the Interstate around five and immediately hit rush hour traffic.

"This is exactly what I wanted to avoid," Adam groaned. "We're going to be stuck on I-95 forever now."

His words proved prophetic. The ladies in the back seat dozed off one by one. Jenny fiddled with the radio and tried to find a song she liked. She finally gave up, staring out of the window at the darkening sky. The long line of cars before and after them required Adam to keep his eyes glued to the road. There wasn't a lot of conversation. Jenny called her son to check on him.

They were nearing Richmond when she dared to mention coffee.

"There's a nice local café right after that exit," she pointed. "We all need a pit stop, I'm sure."

Betty Sue was awake and had a certain look in her eye.

"Can you wait until we reach that big rest area on I-64?" Adam asked. "I want to avoid entering the city."

Half an hour later, they finally spotted a large sign proclaiming the state tourism slogan, 'Virginia is for Lovers'.

"Turn here, turn here." Jenny parroted, lest he miss the big sign. "The visitor center will be closed."

Why did she need it, Adam quizzed.

"Let's make it quick, please."

Jenny asked why he was in such a hurry. Was there something amiss in Pelican Cove?

"No more mishaps on the Isabella?" she queried.

Adam gave a shrug. He had been playing hooky all day and just needed to look in at the police station. Jenny told him that wasn't quite right. He had been on a field trip to question a suspect. Nobody could accuse him of being negligent.

A side of his mouth twisted up in a grudging smile.

"You don't think a prolonged lunch at a fancy restaurant is playing hooky?"

The rest area was huge and they all took the opportunity to stretch their legs. There were vending machines for coffee. Heather undertook the task of getting the hot drinks for them.

Jenny sat at a picnic table, talking longingly of the café she had wanted to visit in Richmond.

"They roast their own beans. It's real coffee, Adam. Not this vending machine stuff."

Adam barely heard her. He stood with his back to them, staring into the mass of towering deciduous trees that lined both sides of the road. Heather began to needle him.

"The whole Senator angle was a dead end, Jenny. You should've known better than to point the finger at such a respected man."

Betty Sue rushed to Jenny's defense. Hadn't Bianca said he was crooked? Not in so many words, Heather argued.

"You should not have believed her," she told Jenny.

Adam trashed his cup and told them he was going for one more.

"That boy thinks too highly of himself," Betty Sue complained. "I say we let him sulk. No need to beat yourself up. You hear me, Jenny?"

Adam came back with two cups. He handed one to Jenny.

"You look chilled to the bone." He tore open a packet of sugar. "Remind me to crank up the heat in the car."

Jenny raised her eyebrows, certain he was mulling over something.

"What is it?"

Without missing a beat, Adam said something that grabbed their attention.

"It could be him, you know." He took a sip. "Senator Worth. He might have killed the guy."

They waited for him to elaborate. He began by mentioning that they were not privy to everything the police discovered on the Isabella. Jenny could not help but roll her eyes at that. Whatever happened to collaboration?

"You were going to sit this one out, remember?" Adam answered the unspoken question. "So it's not as if we were swapping notes."

"Get on with it, man!" Heather nudged. "Why do you suspect Senator Worth?"

Adam took another sip of his coffee and began.

"You know all the video footage around midnight was missing. We had to widen our search area."

Searching every nook and cranny on the Isabella was a mammoth undertaking. Adam's police force would have spent days trying to find something, even if he took on temporary staff. The distance from top to bottom and fore to aft was mind boggling. So they had to be creative.

"We scoured the tapes until the last known location of Dario Lombardi."

Once they found him on the camera, they had chosen a search radius around the spot he had been in.

All three women were listening spellbound, barely paying attention to the cold. The twilight had faded and the lights in the rest area had come on, flooding them in fluorescent brilliance.

"We hit pay dirt." Adam smirked. "There was a damaged cell phone but the technical team was able to determine that it belonged to Dario."

Jenny waited for more. What had the phone revealed? Adam didn't disappoint.

"The last message he sent was to a number that was not saved."

Betty Sue exclaimed she had no idea what he meant.

"You can say it was not written in his diary, Grandma," Heather explained.

"So it must be to a stranger, or someone he had just met." Betty Sue caught on quick. "Do you know who it was?"

Adam shook his head. They were still working on tracing that number. The message had been sent at fifteen minutes after eleven. Dario had set up a meeting with that person.

Jenny's mind raced ahead. Had the poor man paved the way for his own murder?

"Do you think this meeting was on the books for a long time?"

Adam told her it seemed very spur of the moment. Dario wanted to meet the owner of the other phone at midnight.

There was barely an hour between the time he sent the message and the one he proposed.

"The Isabella is big." Adam breathed. "You all know that. It can take a while to get from one end to the other."

How did this tie in with the Senator, Jenny wanted to know.

"The phone could belong to him." Adam gave a shrug. "It's all speculation at the moment, of course. But you never know. He's a slick one. But he has plenty to lose if any of his shady dealings come to light."

Heather thought it was all very obvious. A man in office, or in any position of power would never use his personal phone to do anything underhanded.

"Must be a burner." She yawned. "Yeah, so the Senator stays on our suspect list."

Betty Sue declared they needed to get going.

"I have a feeling there's a crisis back home, waiting for my attention."

Jenny and Heather laughed outright. Adam gave a grudging smile. He put an arm around Betty Sue and led her to the car.

"Why don't you ride shotgun? You can tell me what you are worried about."

"The locals are setting up their stalls today. We are having a dry run tomorrow."

Jenny had totally forgotten about that.

"I think I should pull out of the spring festival. There's no way I can set up my space and make cannolis tomorrow."

Betty Sue told her to relax. It was being taken care of. And she didn't need to participate in the rehearsal. She had been selling food at the spring festival for several years.

"We all ate the cannolis. You don't need to test anything." Betty Sue dismissed.

She had already discussed it with the festival committee. Knowing her, she had probably warned them to go along with anything Jenny did.

"Cook at home and set up a table at the festival."

They were short of the official spaces, since the trucks from out of town had bagged several spots. Betty Sue had come up with a brilliant idea. She was going to place Jenny's desserts at the Welcome Committee table. Anyone who got a ticket would have the option of getting the cannoli at half price.

"But ..." Jenny protested, all her plans of making a profit to help with the renovation collapsing in a second.

Heather told her to relax.

"We already thought of all that. Don't worry, I've been creative with the price."

That meant she had jacked up the price so Jenny could earn a decent amount even with a discount.

"You wily creature!" She punched Heather's arm in a playful manner.

"Billy thought of it. You can thank him."

Jenny was surprised Betty Sue had approved the idea.

"I've seen those frown lines on your forehead, Jenny. Two or three have appeared in the past month. I know I gave you grief over the renovation. This is my way of saying sorry."

Jenny felt her eyes tear up.

"Don't worry at all," Heather soothed. "The café will do a roaring business once we reopen. And that mural! That's going to make you famous!"

Adam surprised her by agreeing with them. He hoped she was ready with a revamped menu.

"Just keep the chicken salad. And the chocolate chip cookies and banana muffins."

Two hours later, they entered the city of Virginia Beach. They were all hungry. Adam proposed taking a quick stop to eat something.

"How about that place on the waterfront?" he asked Jenny. "The one that has those really big cheeseburgers you like?"

"We're in the home stretch. Are you sure this is fine?"

Adam's stomach gave a big growl, making them all burst into laughter.

They parked in a public lot and walked down a block to the cafe. Only two tables were occupied and Jenny ordered chips and salsa to get them started. She just needed to eat something right away.

Betty Sue asked for pasta while the others got bacon cheeseburgers with fries.

The food arrived and Adam asked for a large coffee to go.

"Do you really expect any trouble at the spring fest?" Jenny asked him.

Adam told them he was prepared. A patrol car would be on hand to deter any skirmishes.

"Let's hope the locals behave. My first priority is to figure out who murdered Dario Lombardi. Maybe the Isabella will leave our shore then."

Chapter 14

Jenny broke her own rule the next morning and baked blueberry muffins. She made a spiced honey butter to go with them. The eggs came next and got the royal treatment with chives and sharp cheddar.

Star was rubbing her eyes when she came down for breakfast.

"What's this? You're going to tire yourself out, sweetie."

Jenny brushed off her concern and plated some of the eggs. The toast was ready in a minute and they ate quickly with an eye on the clock. The deliveries took longer than usual. Almost every customer commented on the food.

"Smells real good," one of them said. "Can't wait for the café to reopen."

"What's this?" a crotchety old gentleman grumbled. "These don't look like my eggs."

Jenny explained she had just embellished them a bit. He was not happy. He preferred them plain.

"You can't please everyone." Star laughed as they got back in the car.

They reached the café and dispensed the remaining food. Star went in to resume work on her mural. She wanted Jenny to have a look.

"What do you think?" Her uncertainty was splashed across her face. "Is it good enough?" She squeezed the dirty rag she was holding. "We can always just paint it over, you know."

Jenny was aghast.

"Don't you dare! This is ... spectacular! I don't have the proper words to describe it. And anything I say is not going to be enough. Just wait until we reopen. Every tourist who walks in will want to own one of your paintings."

Placated for the moment, Star picked up a brush and began mixing some paint. Jenny left her alone, wondering what had brought on this self doubt in her aunt.

The deck was bathed in dappled sunlight, providing questionable warmth. It was another cold and windy day and spring seemed to be hesitating at the door.

Jenny fixed herself a tiny cup of coffee and sat down, putting her leg up on the chair before her. She had barely taken a sip when the man calling himself Quinn came up. He was dressed in khakis and a checks shirt, with a denim jacket slung over one shoulder.

"Howdy!"

"Yes?" Jenny didn't care to hide her irritation.

The conceited private investigator was the last person she wanted to see.

"What's the latest?" he asked without preamble, pulling out a chair and sitting right in front of her. "The family is asking what progress the police have made."

Jenny suggested he go to the police station and talk to the Sheriff. Quinn replied he wasn't going to do that.

"You are going to be my point of contact in this town."

"But why?" she bristled. "I don't work for you, okay? You got some nerve, coming here uninvited and making demands of me."

Quinn's expression turned menacing. Did she have no sense?

"I suggest you come clean and tell me what you know. Do I have to spell it out?" He leaned forward, placed his hand behind his back and pulled out a gun. Jenny was shocked when he placed it on the table between them. "Nothing good ever came of opposing the Lombardis."

Jenny felt her legs turn wobbly but she kept up her bravado.

"You can't come to my property and threaten me. There's a law against that."

Quinn laughed, his lips raised in a mocking manner.

"Laws don't apply to some people."

Jenny wanted him gone at the earliest.

"Look, you don't frighten me, okay? The only reason I'm telling you this is because of Dario." She paused as a sudden rush of emotion invaded her. The Lombardi family must be grieving. They had lost a son, after all. "Dario had an argument with Harry Campbell. I'm not sure what it was about but Harry wasn't happy."

"Who told you this?"

Some instinct made Jenny hold back.

"I can't remember. Some woman in town. I come across dozens of people in a day, Quinn." She sneered. "You're an investigator. I've given you a big clue. You should be able to work with that."

He sprang up, gave her a nod and was gone before she could expel a breath.

"Hey! Watch it, man!"

Quinn had collided with Jason who was coming up the steps.

"You forgot something." Jenny called out, unwilling to move an inch while the gun was on the table. She just hoped Jason wouldn't spot it but it was too late.

"What's this?" He rushed to Jenny's side and placed his hands on her shoulders.

She heaved a sigh of relief, glad of his support.

Quinn took his time walking back. He picked up the gun and tucked it in his waistband.

"You better not have threatened my wife," Jason warned in an icy tone. "The Sheriff will put you behind bars for carrying a weapon."

Quinn flashed his teeth in a menacing grin.

"Not if I have a license for it."

Jason argued that didn't allow him to use it as a tool for intimidation. Quinn gave him a mock salute and left without a word.

In the next moment, Jenny was in her husband's arms, shaking.

"I'm sorry. I'm sorry. He just turned up all of a sudden."

Jason kissed her forehead, assuring her it was not her fault. Then he pulled out his phone and called someone. Jenny said nothing as he talked to Billy first and then to Adam.

"We're getting a restraining order," he announced. "If you see that man again, you are to call Adam at once."

Jenny chose discretion and said nothing. She was glad there was an army of people ready to defend her.

"Shall we go for a walk?"

Jason nodded solemnly. They were quiet as they strolled along the boardwalk, neither willing to say what was uppermost in their mind. Finally, Jenny wondered what he was doing at the café in the middle of the morning.

"I thought I might grab a bite before heading to a meeting in the city."

Did she have any extra muffins for him?

They went back to the deck and Jenny heated up a muffin in the microwave she had set up on a ledge. Jason was quiet as he spread some butter on his muffin.

"Don't worry. I'll be careful. Quinn ... he's all bluster. There's no need to be afraid of him."

Jason's gaze travelled over the water to the grand ship anchored a mile out.

"These people don't follow any rules, Jenny. The sooner they are gone, the better it will be for all of us."

They hugged again and Jenny told Jason to get going. The Magnolias would be there soon. And Star was inside, along with the workmen. She was perfectly safe.

Jenny huddled in her sweater and folded her arms, reviewing what had happened since the night of the party. With a start, she remembered the phone number Adam had mentioned. Had the police found out more?

She sent off a message, asking if his team had found something. Part of her fully expected to be ignored or chastised. So she was surprised when Adam sent a proper response.

Heather's guess had been right. The phone number that Dario had messaged belonged to a disposable phone. They would try to figure out who it belonged to but it was almost impossible. All they had found out was there had been no other communication from that number, other than the message Dario sent.

Jenny lapsed into thought, trying to understand what that meant. The phone had been purchased for a purpose. Had that been talking to Dario to set up the fatal appointment? Maybe he had also not been aware of the identity of the phone's owner.

A babble of raised voices reached her. Heather arrived, accompanied by Betty Sue with her knitting bag slung over her shoulder. Molly was just behind, lugging a stack of books.

Star came out, looking flustered.

"You can't allow this, Betty Sue," she cried. "Are you going to do nothing? If ever there was a time for you to exercise your power, this is it."

Betty Sue settled herself at one end of a long table and pulled out her knitting.

"You can't see the forest for the trees, Star. None of you can. What do you expect me to do? Shut down the spring festival? That has never happened in the history of Pelican Cove."

Her needles began clacking furiously as she shook her head.

"I'm not going to be responsible for breaking tradition." She glared at the ship out in the ocean. "We all saw the result of doing that!"

Jenny understood she was referring to the ship being jinxed.

"What's wrong? Sounds like a matter of life and death."

Star told her she wasn't far off the mark. The spring festival was supposed to have a dry run that day. All the vendors had gathered at the spot. That included the business owners from town who were setting up their stalls and the food truck owners who had driven down from various locations.

"Okay." Jenny encouraged her to continue. "How'd that go?"

Heather interrupted to declare it was a disaster.

"Things were quiet at first. It was the lull before the storm, if you ask me."

There had been an electrical failure, maybe a short circuit. Sparks flew and a vendor's stall caught fire. Fortunately, the man in the adjoining booth saw it and used a fire extinguisher.

"Everyone's fine then?" Jenny breathed. "No mishaps, I hope."

Molly looked up from her book, finally entering the conversation. The fire was just the beginning. One of the locals accused a food truck owner of drawing more power than allowed. All the other booth owners banded together, agreeing that the food truck people had overloaded a circuit, resulting in the fire.

Jenny's mouth dropped open. Clearly, they needed to put out a different kind of fire.

"All these Main Street store owners were against the outsiders anyway," Heather added. "Someone floated the theory that it was done on purpose."

The argument had reached a crescendo and escalated until fists were about to fly. The police had stepped in, having to physically separate the two sides.

"Was the patrol car on site like Adam said?"

Betty Sue told her having those two deputies on hand had probably saved the day. The Sheriff was not happy and had warned he would put an end to the festival if peace wasn't restored.

"Can he do that?" Jenny was curious.

"The town council reigns supreme," Betty Sue ordained. "But life is precious. If these fools continue to fight, we'll have no choice but to shut the festival down."

Chapter 15

Jenny heated the remaining muffins and offered them to her friends.

"Try the butter. Let me know what you think."

It was the right distraction. Everyone took turns slathering the butter on their muffins. Jenny warmed the coffee and fixed a cup for herself. She was still a bit jittery inspite of Jason's assurances. Why had he turned up at the exact moment when Quinn was there? The Lombardis would not harm her husband, would they?

Molly got up to get coffee, giving Jenny a speculative look.

"You look shaken. Are you hiding something from us?"

Out poured the whole incident with the slimy private investigator. Star was indignant.

"I was right inside when all this happened. Why didn't you call out, sweetie?" She mentioned the men who were working in the kitchen. "He needed to know you were not alone."

What would any of them have done if Quinn decided to use his gun? Jenny didn't voice that, simply apologizing to Star.

"I didn't realize ... it was a shock. What can I say? Totally unexpected and out of left field."

Betty Sue's eyes had clouded in concern. This was one more reason they needed to get rid of the Isabella. Jenny sensed the older ladies were spiraling and flashed Heather a helpless look. She needed her to step in.

"Any news from Adam?" Heather took the cue. "What are the police doing, huh?"

Jenny had completely forgotten about the phone. She told them what she had learned from Adam.

"So you were right. It was indeed a burner phone."

Molly's eyes had widened and the book she was perusing slipped from her grasp and fell on the table.

"You know who I saw buying a burner phone a few days ago?" She didn't wait for a response. "Wilson!"

"From the garage?" Jenny confirmed.

"Yes, yes. Peter Wilson. You know who I mean, Jenny."

Before Jenny could gather her thoughts, Heather started talking about his background and his connection to the Bellini family.

"Who was that guy who came in here the other day? One who said he was Petunia's cousin?"

"Tony Bellini?" Jenny frowned.

What did he have to do with the matter at hand?

"Peter Wilson worked for the Bellini family," Heather summarized. "He came to Pelican Cove at their behest to keep an eye on Petunia and protect her. And we know from this Tony guy that the Bellinis were also hoping to set up a casino here."

Jenny vaguely remembered the Senator mentioning something like that.

"Go on," she prompted.

"So ... the Bellinis missed the bus but they can't have been happy. What if they ordered Wilson to get rid of the Lombardis? Killing Dario could be a warning. Get out of Pelican Cove or else ..."

Jenny didn't agree. Wilson may have been dispatched to Pelican Cove to keep an eye on Petunia but he had left his old life behind. He was just a garage owner now. An honest, small town business owner with a family.

"You really think he's working for the Bellinis again?"

Molly believed it was possible. The disposable phone might have been to lure Dario or talk to him. It could easily be destroyed later.

Jenny pointed out the flaw in her reasoning. Dario was the one who had sent the message. But he could have obtained the number from Wilson any way, Molly argued. Wilson might have given it to him in town or on the ship. What if Wilson had given him some handwritten note, spurring him into action? Something he could not ignore?

"Like a more attractive business proposition, maybe?" Heather added. "Or a time sensitive issue that had to be addressed at once."

Jenny gave a spontaneous laugh. Heather's personality had changed a lot since her association with Billy. It hadn't happened overnight but bit by bit, her outlook on life and her approach to a problem had changed, making her apply her mind more.

"That's Billy talking. Money's always the first angle he considers." She sighed. "And he's right most of the time."

Heather endured some good natured ribbing after that. Molly tapped the desk sometime later.

"So when do we leave? I can take the afternoon off."

Jenny didn't catch her meaning right away.

"Are we going somewhere?"

Molly rolled her eyes. They needed to go talk to Wilson, of course. And they were not letting Jenny go there on her own.

Jenny glanced at her watch and gave a cry. The lunch hour was approaching and she was already late.

"I need to go home right away. Will you come along, Heather? I need help."

Molly and Jenny made plans to meet on the deck around two in the afternoon.

The next couple of hours passed quickly. There were a few more complaints from the customers. When would they get a hot meal? Jenny made a joke about all of them staging a protest at the Cohen Construction office.

She and Star ate their sandwiches on the deck and waited for Molly. Heather had gone back to the inn, bragging about the pot of soup she had started in the slow cooker that morning.

"Why don't you come and have a bowl? Aren't you tired of the same old chicken sandwich?"

"I happen to like them!" Jenny protested. "And by the way, I'm having a pimento cheese sandwich today, just so you know. And chips."

Molly arrived in a rush.

"Am I late? There was a big line at the checkout counter."

Star urged them to be careful. Jenny wondered if they should call ahead.

"No, no. We want the element of surprise." Molly said.

They set off in Jenny's car. There was some lingering warmth from the sun but the breeze was making it feel colder.

"I feel bad about this," Jenny confessed as they neared the bridge. "Are we making too much of nothing? I mean, this is Wilson. We know him! He's been protective of me."

Molly thought it didn't hurt to be careful. What if the Bellini family threatened his family or raked up his past? Wilson would have to do their bidding.

They pulled up at the garage. Wilson was working on a vintage car. He wiped his hands on a dirty grease rag and came to greet them.

"Hey Jenny! Car giving you trouble? You're not due for a servicing until next month."

She assured him the car was in perfect condition. Unwilling to launch into an interrogation, she pointed at the maroon Thunderbird he had been tinkering with.

"New project?"

Peter Wilson laughed and gave a shrug. It was something to keep him busy.

"Vintage car rally coming up in Richmond in the summer. I hope to have this baby ready by then. I'll give you a ride once she's ready."

He led them to his office and sent his young secretary to make coffee. She came back with steaming mugs and a plate of doughnuts.

Jenny found herself reaching for the sweet treat.

"Okay then." Wilson took a big bite out of a jelly doughnut. "The wife can't say I wasn't pleasant. Out with it, Miss Jenny. What's bothering you?"

All her doubts resurfaced and she felt a blush stealing over her cheeks.

"I'm, uh, trying to figure out what happened to Dario Lombardi. He was nice to me, you know." She paused, watching his blank face. "Had you met him before coming here?"

He frowned, then his face cleared in comprehension.

"Oh, you mean when I was in New Jersey? No, no. He was a lot younger than me. I never met him, even after they anchored off shore and he visited town. And I didn't get a chance to talk to him on the night of the party either."

Molly's expression was skeptical.

Jenny thought of what was most relevant. Adam had asked the Senator about his whereabouts at midnight.

"Can you tell me what you were doing from say, 11:30 to 12:30 that night? I am trying to verify someone's statement and I wonder if you were around them."

If Wilson thought it was a bald faced lie, he didn't show it. He had been with Betty Sue at the time of the toast and later during the fireworks. She was free to ask her.

He stirred sugar in his coffee and tapped his spoon on the rim.

"I didn't get a good start in life. My circumstances were less than ideal, Miss Jenny. But I left all that behind." He blinked. "I have no desire to go back to it. My life and my family's wellbeing is too valuable."

Jenny let him speak.

"You saw that car I'm working on? I'm living a dream. One I never want to wake up from. Colluding with the Lombardis or the Bellinis is out of question."

Jenny almost sighed in relief. But here was a man who was very familiar with the life of crime. He could provide useful insight.

"What do you think of all this? The way the murder was committed, the timing ..."

Wilson responded eagerly. It was a crime of passion according to him, done without any planning. Strangling was not how the mafia operated. Nothing about the way Dario was killed indicated a crime family was involved.

"I hear the buzz. Can't avoid it."

Did he mean he still had friends from his old life? Jenny could not blame him for that.

"This kid was a Casanova of sorts. A rich playboy. He suddenly thought of this venture to impress the old man and went all out. A lot of money was poured in, a lot. And he convinced his brother and sister to invest with him. Primo is not pleased!"

"It's a sound business idea." Jenny gave a dry laugh. "We just want them to go anchor somewhere else."

Wilson thought Dario was not skilled enough to manage everything on his own.

"He wanted to play boss but was ill equipped. Never done anything right in his life, apparently. Primo thought the only way to keep little brother in line was to keep an eye on him." He grabbed another doughnut from the plate. "I think the other two Lombardi kids were here to babysit Dario."

Molly almost cut him off.

"I'm looking for a disposable phone. Can you recommend one over the other?"

Wilson seemed confused.

"I saw you at the store the other day, buying one of those tiny phones that already come with a number."

Was that a flash of annoyance in Peter Wilson's eyes? Jenny couldn't tell.

"Oh, that. My niece is coming to visit for the spring festival. Wife's sister asked us to keep tabs on her." He snorted. "It's a shackle disguised as a gift."

Jenny praised him for being clever. Parents needed to be subtle these days.

"The things we do for our kids," she chuckled.

They left the garage and started back. Molly was looking disappointed.

"I'm sorry. That was a waste of time."

Jenny told her she was being premature.

"We need to talk to Betty Sue to confirm what he said."

Chapter 16

Jenny felt weary by the time she went back home. Craving the comfort of a hot drink, she fixed herself a cup of hot chocolate, adding a dollop of whipped cream on top. It had turned chilly outside and she cupped her hands around the thick stoneware mug, leaned back on the couch and put her feet up on the coffee table. Her mind was blissfully blank as she sipped her drink and she must have dozed off.

She woke up with a start when she felt a tug. Jason was stooping down, gently removing the mug from her hands.

"Hey honey."

"What time is it?" Jenny sat up, rubbing her eyes. "I haven't even started dinner yet."

Jason told her to relax.

"Why don't we go out? You can pick the place."

Jenny's first thought was the Steakhouse but she immediately discarded it. She would rather avoid the place until she squared things with Harry Campbell.

"Aren't you tired? A drive seems daunting. It's turned quite chilly."

Jason sat down beside her and agreed. At times such as this, Jenny missed the convenience of having a bunch of takeout options at hand.

"Don't we have those food trucks in town? I thought they are supposed to offer many exotic options. Thai food was mentioned."

Jenny wasn't sure if they were operational. The latest skirmish between them and the locals had not ended well. She had no wish to call Betty Sue for an update or get more gossip. But Jason's words made her think.

"You've given me an idea. Are you really thinking of Thai food?"

She had a bottle of red curry paste in the pantry. As always, Jason got in the spirit of things and they rooted around the fridge, making a pile of the vegetables they had on hand.

"Red curry, rice and chicken satay." Jenny declared. "How does that sound?"

Jason was worried if she was up to it.

"I thought you were exhausted."

"You'll help me, won't you? I just can't bear the thought of dressing up and going out, being in a public space. Here, I can just wear my sweats and rustle up something."

They were both of the same mind. She set Jason to chopping the veggies and marinated the chicken. Less than an hour later, they loaded their plates with fragrant jasmine rice, spicy red curry and chicken grilled on skewers, satay style.

"Don't forget the sauce!" Jenny pointed to the bowl of dipping sauce that went with the chicken.

Jason had started a fire in the living room. They each flopped down on a chair, put their feet up on ottomans and plunged their forks in.

"This is delicious!" Jason spoke after half his plate was empty. "Have you considered adding it to the café menu?"

Jenny had thought of several options. Having a curry day when she would cook a different one a certain day of the week. Or dedicating an entire week a month to a different cuisine.

"It's a bit much. For now, let's just enjoy this." She plunged her skewer in the creamy peanut sauce.

Jason had opened a bottle of Sauvignon Blanc. They finished eating and cuddled on the sofa, sipping wine.

"I think we need to get away for a bit, Jenny."

She brought up the cherry blossoms. Jason told her he wasn't talking about just a couple of days. They would spend a weekend in Washington DC whenever she wanted. He meant a longer break. At least a month.

"Actually, I was thinking we could take a sabbatical and tour Europe. You liked spending summer in the South of France, didn't you?" He planted a kiss on her head. "We could go to Tuscany, sample some great Italian food. And Greece."

Jenny couldn't hold back her laughter. She was touched Jason was thinking like that. But it was a pipe dream.

"I think I have to stay in Pelican Cove this summer, once the café reopens. The natives are unhappy. And have you seen the astronomical figure the Cohens are charging us?"

"But you have toiled so much all your life. This is the time to let loose. Once Nicky gives us grandkids, we won't have the heart to be away from them."

Jenny shook her head. Nick didn't even have a steady girlfriend.

"You just can't imagine not playing detective," Jason teased. "Admit it. Especially since Adam has taken you under his wing."

"That's not correct. He has ordered me to stay out of the investigation this time."

But was she doing that, Jason grinned. Jenny sidestepped the question.

"The Isabella is having a really bad impact on the town. Look at all these fights breaking out. Maybe the negative vibes are making people jittery."

"Superstition."

"Even so, that ship and the Lombardis are disturbing our equilibrium. I wish they would leave soon."

Jason told her that a certain amount of crime was inevitable. Pelican Cove had faced its share of murders.

"What have you found?" He quirked an eyebrow. "Hands off or not, I can't believe you are completely isolated from this business. Surely you must have a theory?"

Jenny toyed with her empty glass, taking time to reply. The police themselves didn't know much, she told Jason. There was a big dearth of evidence. All Adam knew was the approximate time Dario had taken his last breath, the way he died and the message.

"What message?"

"The one Dario sent just before he died, to a burner phone."

Jason encouraged her to elaborate.

"We know zilch. Adam believes Dario was going to meet someone at midnight but there are a lot of unanswered questions."

Where was Dario meeting this mysterious person? Was it on the pier or on the ship itself, where they had found his damaged phone. Had he crushed it under his foot on purpose or had the other person done it? Maybe it was accidental.

Jason nodded along. All of these questions were valid and needed to be answered.

"You must have some suspects."

With a deep sigh, Jenny brought up Harry Campbell. Jason immediately protested, just like she had expected.

"My Dad and Harry were good friends. Say what you will, Jenny, Harry Campbell doesn't have a mean bone in his body."

He hadn't seen how Harry was treating her nowadays.

"I've become persona non grata with him. All because I won fair and square in that tasting contest. And I don't believe losing one contract is going to impact the Steakhouse so much. It's his ego that's hurt."

"Losing to a woman?" Jason winked. "That's not impossible. He belongs to a different generation."

Jenny was astounded. Was Jason defending Harry?

"No, no. What I mean is, sure, he'll sulk for a few days. He might even be rude to you. But Harry Campbell taking someone's life? That I will not believe."

Jenny gave a shrug. She liked Harry and hoped he was innocent. Having a stalwart like him commit such a heinous crime would really shake the foundation of the town.

"There are the Bellinis, of course. Do you believe they are capable of this crime?"

Jason agreed with her. But the animosity between the Lombardis and the Bellinis went back years. Why now?

"Senator Worth told us the Bellinis wanted to set up a casino on the water too. And Tony confirmed it. Killing Dario might chase off the Lombardis and give them the chance they missed."

"And you think they hired Wilson to do it?" Jason surprised her.

"He's not involved in any of this, he says. According to him, he's no longer working for the Bellinis." She paused. "But what if they coerce him?"

She told him about the disposable phone. He hadn't denied it when Molly confronted him.

"He knew he couldn't." Jason replied. "You would not doubt Molly. And how many people buy that kind of a phone on a day to day basis? Mr. Williams would surely remember it, catching Wilson out in his lie. So he played smart, I think."

"The niece was a complete fabrication, then?"

Jason shook his head. Peter Wilson did have a niece. It was entirely plausible that the niece would visit them for the spring festival.

The fire was dying. Jason stood up and stretched.

"Are you going for your walk?"

Jenny shook her head. She was too full and didn't want to move from her spot.

"I'm taking a break tonight. Why don't you stoke the fire and come back here?"

Jason did that, then went into the kitchen in search of dessert. He returned with two bowls of chocolate ice cream, topped with strawberry sauce. It was left over from the last batch of cannolis.

"Let's not forget the Senator. He's rich and powerful. And I don't know how to say this, Jenny. He probably has people who are ready to die for him. Literally."

Jenny was certain the Senator had been instrumental in paving the way for the Lombardis. And there was no doubt he had been paid well for his assistance.

"He could even be an investor. The Isabella cost an arm and a leg, apparently."

Why would he kill the hand that fed him? They both agreed that suspecting the Senator did not make sense.

"But I can't forget the look in his eyes, Jason. He's crooked."

The police needed to find more evidence so they could eliminate some of these suspects. Jason brought up the Lombardis.

"What about family dynamics? Did the siblings get along?"

Jenny had no firsthand knowledge. Bianca was formidable, so was Primo. Dario had been soft with Jenny but he could be intimidating too.

"Quite an eccentric bunch. And there's the old man. According to the grapevine, Dario was not very smart." Jenny frowned. "Wilson says he wasn't as successful as the other two."

But the entire family had put in a lot of money in the venture. They stood to lose a lot if the casino failed. What if it succeeded though? All of them would earn millions.

Jenny wondered if it had all been a power struggle. Jason licked his spoon, his eyes wide as he considered her theory.

"You think Dario got too big for his boots?"

Chapter 17

Jenny was in an upbeat mood the next morning. She hummed an old show tune as she scrambled the eggs and packed the boxes. The sun was climbing up the sky when she got into her car to make the deliveries. A warm front was moving in and the weather forecast promised a high of seventy. She was glad she had taken the time to relax with Jason the previous evening. There was a bounce in her step that had been missing for a while.

I'm going to tackle that foreman today, she told herself. And I'm ready to visit the company's office to give them an ultimatum. Having a solid plan cheered her up. She dropped off the breakfast boxes, rushing to the café.

At least she didn't have to visit Philomena Ryder that morning. The woman was a chatty Cathy. Her back was much better and she had begun moving about. Star had seen her in town so Jenny didn't feel she had to hand deliver the woman's breakfast.

Captain Charlie sat on the deck, reading a newspaper. He greeted Jenny in his usual spirited manner.

"You're looking chipper."

Jenny beamed and handed him a muffin.

"I'll fix your coffee right away."

He waved a hand at the people milling on the deck and the boardwalk.

"Take care of them first. I'm not going anywhere."

It didn't take her long to dispense with the boxes and bags she had already packed. Star was inside, cleaning her brushes.

"Care to join us?" she peeped in. "Captain Charlie's here."

The two women sat down before him with their coffee.

"How's it going?" Jenny asked him. "Don't you have a charter today?"

She was a bit worried about him. Based on the grapevine, he had invested a lot of money in fixing his old boat. And he almost bought a new one. All because the Lombardis had promised he would have sole rights to ferry people to and from shore.

It was the slow season and tourists were in short supply. Captain Charlie ate the last bit of muffin and wiped his hands on a napkin.

"Are you worried about me, Missy?"

His eyes misted.

"The casino's starting up in a day or two. They have done a big advertising campaign in Atlantic City. And the engineer on the ship said they are bringing busloads of people from a senior center tomorrow."

He would be making plenty of trips and would get paid at a handsome rate as promised.

"Fingers crossed," Star said. "You'll tell us if you need any help?"

Jenny was thinking the same. She would ask Jason and Billy to take Captain Charlie out for a drink in a couple of days. He would be more open with them.

She glanced at the food on the makeshift table set up on the deck and realized something.

"Philomena! She never showed."

Star wanted to know what she meant. Jenny pointed at the extra bag, containing the box of scrambled eggs and two muffins, just as Philomena had ordered.

"Didn't you say you saw her in town yesterday?" She frowned. "Oh yes, Molly also mentioned she came to the library."

Jenny explained how she had thought the woman was well now and would come to the café herself. She hadn't been happy laid up in bed.

"Sounds like a misunderstanding, sweetie." Star clucked. "Did you confirm this with her? You are positive she was going to come to the café herself?"

Jenny shook her head. She had just assumed. Then she thought of another scenario. What if her back was worse? Philomena might be in bed, unable to move again.

"I'm going to check up on her."

Star went back in to resume her painting. Captain Charlie planned to hang around a little longer. Jenny urged him to help himself to more coffee.

"Poor thing. She eats dinner early so she's very hungry by the time breakfast rolls around. I better leave now."

There was a reason Jenny had been looking out for Philomena that morning. Jason's words from the previous night had stuck with her. He was so sure Harry Campbell was a good man. Jenny wanted to ask her to think harder. Had she really heard Harry's voice, arguing with Dario like she claimed. Could it have been somebody else?

The sun warmed her back and she picked up her step, reaching Philomena's house in minutes. This time she didn't even try knocking on the front door. Instead, she walked around the house on the paved stones leading to the patch of garden at the back.

"Hello!" she called through a window, then had a moment of uncertainty.

What if the old woman was asleep? She wouldn't like being disturbed.

One glance at her watch told Jenny the day was getting on. A gasp escaped her when she reached the back door. It was open.

She climbed the two stairs and stepped onto a tiny porch. What she saw inside left her cold. Broken plates and glasses were strewn on the floor. There was a single shoe amidst the debris.

"What in the world…" Jenny muttered to herself and rushed in, afraid for Philomena.

Her blood ran cold when she saw two feet on the ground, jutting out from behind a center island. Why was the woman sleeping on the floor?

A rare voice of reason made her stop in her tracks. She retraced her steps and went out. Pulling her cell phone from her bag, she called Adam.

"I'm at Philomena Ryder's house. You should come here soon."

She sat on the steps, waiting, praying she was just being silly. Adam would berate her for wasting valuable police resources but it wouldn't matter if Philomena was fine.

Sirens approached and Jenny ran around the house to the front. A squad car came to a screeching stop and Adam jumped out.

"Over here." Jenny pointed. "The back door."

She ran after him but came to a halt when he flung out a hand to thwart her.

"Stay here until I check things out. Please, Jenny."

She complied, eager to avoid any more delay. She just wanted to know Philomena was safe. Her heart thudded in her chest as she waited. It seemed like an eternity when Adam came out, his face grim.

"Sorry, Jenny. We're too late."

She felt herself crumble but Adam was by her in a trice, grabbing her arms, holding her up.

"It's my fault. I forgot! How could I do that, Adam? She would be alive if I'd come to deliver her breakfast like I've been doing. Her back was out, you see? And she was on pain killers, I bet. The poor woman must have slipped."

"Hey, hey ..." Adam tried to stop her. "Look at me, Jenny. Get a hold of yourself."

He made her sit on the tiny back porch.

"She was murdered, Jenny. Nothing you could have done."

"But that's impossible."

Adam told her he had checked out the crime scene. Based on his experience, he was pretty sure someone had taken her life.

More sirens wailed in the distance. An ambulance arrived, followed by more of Adam's deputies. He bid one of them to give her a ride.

"I have to take care of all this, Jenny. We'll catch up later."

She had to tell him.

"Philomena heard Harry Campbell arguing with Dario Lombardi. They almost came to blows!"

Adam didn't say a word, just tipped his head to the side, signaling his deputy to take her to the waiting car.

"Do you think that's relevant?" Jenny cried, craning her neck backwards, trying to keep his attention.

"Later, Jenny." Adam replied softly.

Jenny's mind was in turmoil as the car sped to the café. She was sure Harry had found out and chosen to silence the woman. But how did he know she had seen him fight with Dario?

The Magnolias were assembled on the deck, grumbling over their coffee.

"Microwaving is not the same." Heather accosted Jenny. "You lose the taste once you reheat." She was on a roll.

Molly sprang up and took Jenny's arm.

"Hush." She warned Heather. "Just be quiet for a sec."

"What did I ..." Heather looked up from stirring her cup and came face to face with Jenny. "What's wrong?"

Tears flowed down her cheeks. Trying to hold back her sobs, Jenny told them about Philomena.

"Another murder!" Betty Sue flushed. "I won't say I'm surprised."

Star heard the commotion and came out, holding a wet paint brush, her smock spattered in a myriad colors.

"The foreman was looking for you ... Jenny?" She thrust the brush in a pocket and leapt forward, taking her niece in her arms. "What's wrong, sweetie?"

Molly had heated a cup of coffee for her. She stirred in more sugar than usual and urged Jenny to drink it.

"I feel helpless." She sighed.

They sat like that for a while, too shocked to comment much. Heather got up after a while.

"Why don't we check out the spring festival?"

Jenny had forgotten all about it.

"The cannolis!" she exclaimed. "I'd planned to go home after breakfast and make a batch, so they could be ready for the evening."

Betty Sue told her to take it easy. She would square things with the festival committee.

"But we still need to have lunch." Heather argued. "Let's go there and try the food trucks. It will get your mind off things."

Jenny didn't think she could forget the scene of devastation at Philomena's house. And those feet ... now she knew they had belonged to a dead woman. The image would stay with her forever.

Molly decided to join them. She just requested they make a pit stop at the library first. Jenny went along.

There was a sizable crowd at the festival. More than half were locals or people visiting them from other towns on the Eastern Shore. Jenny recognized quite a few faces, having come across them over the years.

"Tacos!" Heather pointed at a black truck with a huge, colorful taco painted on it.

The smell of adobo seasoning and meat roasting on the grill assailed their senses as they grew near.

"We're having some of that!" Heather declared, then moved on to a Thai food truck.

Molly found a table for them under the marquee and Jenny sat, still in a daze. Soon, the table before her was spread in an array of dishes.

"Tacos, Pad Thai, chicken and waffles, pizza ..." Heather beamed. "Not a bad selection."

Jenny could hear the desperation in her friend's voice. Heather's eyes were bright. She was trying very hard to distract Jenny. Molly had withdrawn into herself and was quieter than usual.

"She liked to read to the children ... Philomena." Her breath hitched. "For story hour."

Jenny took a clean fork and plunged it into the noodles. She made a conscious effort to eat them and was surprised to find she was hungry.

"You got a good selection, Heather."

It was her turn to coax the others to start eating. Most of the food was delicious. Jenny hoped the people in town would acknowledge that and be open to new experiences.

"That guy looks familiar." Heather looked up, chewing on a drumstick. "You see that tattoo on his neck? A ship's anchor, surrounded by daisies. Unusual, isn't it?"

Jenny followed her gaze and spotted the young man.

"Of course. That's Dario's man. Stuck to him like a leech."

"Must be his bodyguard," Molly offered.

Jenny wondered why she had never thought of that.

"So the Isabella's crew is allowed to come ashore, I guess. See that girl he's with? She was serving food on the night of the party."

Heather's sharp eyes noticed a lot. There was trouble in paradise.

'She's almost in tears. Think he's harassing her?" She pushed her chair back and yelled. "Hey! Hey you!"

Jenny shushed her and placed a hand on her lap. The man had raised his voice and she wanted to hear what he was saying.

"You're the biggest fool I know! Do you have any idea how dangerous these people are? I'm warning you, girl. Better keep your trap shut!"

Chapter 18

The foreman had encouraging news for Jenny but she barely heard a word he said. She couldn't sit still once she went home and slaved in the kitchen, turning out batches of cannolis. She had promised the festival committee and wouldn't go back on her word.

Barb Norton was thrilled to receive her call.

"I was going to talk Molly into baking some brownies for the ticket counter. But this is great news."

"Can you send someone to pick them up?"

Barb promised one of the volunteers would be at Seaview in thirty minutes.

Jenny waited until a young boy she had seen around town arrived to pick up the stuff. Then she trudged up to her room and sat in the window, gazing into nothingness. Philomena's voice was ringing in her ears and her face appeared whenever she closed her eyes. Had a random comment resulted in the poor woman's death?

Star peeped in some time after the sun had set.

"Why are you sitting in the dark, sweetie?"

Jenny jumped down and gave a wan smile.

"Time to start dinner. It's just us. Jason had to go into the city and he's gonna be late. May even stay there because he has an early morning meeting tomorrow."

Star told her she was making chicken noodle soup. And she had rustled up a quick cobbler with some peaches they had frozen over the summer.

Aunt and niece sat in the living room as the soup simmered, watching Golden Girls reruns. Star excused herself after dinner. Jenny tried to read a book but found herself staring into the fireplace. Finally, she jumped up and laced her sneakers, ready to go for a long walk.

She went farther than usual and had turned around when Tank came barreling toward her. He placed his paws on her chest, drool hanging from his mouth.

"Down, you beast!" Jenny wrapped her arms around him. "You're slobbering all over me."

Adam stood a few feet away. He threw a stick in the distance and Tank scampered off. Jenny set off toward her house, listening to Adam give her an update about how things had unfolded.

"Did you manage to meet Harry Campbell?"

"I did. He was at the Steakhouse but agreed to come in to see me." He turned to Jenny. "Harry did talk to Dario that night. But we could corroborate what he said via the tapes, Jenny."

Harry had been talking to someone else around the time Dario disappeared. The cameras had captured that. Adam had gone the extra mile and contacted the person Harry had been with. The man confirmed they had a couple of drinks and talked about business.

"Could he be covering for him?"

Adam thought that was unlikely. The man owned a restaurant in upstate New York. They were swapping notes, from one business owner to another. He was meeting Harry for the first time.

"That man has never come to the Eastern Shore before this. And I doubt Harry ever made it to upstate New York."

Jenny was disappointed. Harry Campbell was the only sure lead she had. Was she missing something? Suddenly, she remembered the conversation she had overheard at the spring festival.

"I spotted Dario's bodyguard earlier today. He was talking to a girl who works on the ship. It was very suspicious."

Adam didn't say much but she could tell he was skeptical.

"He was threatening her, Adam." Jenny stressed. "I'm sure the girl knows something, or she was at the wrong place at the wrong time." She huffed. "Maybe this young guy killed Philomena."

Adam told her the police were still in the early stages of the investigation. Jenny asked him about the burner phone. Did he have any new information on that?

"It's not that easy."

He was frustrated but was trying to be patient with her. The phone could belong to anyone. There was no record and it was almost impossible to figure out who had bought it. They could not assume it was a person in town.

But had he talked to Wilson yet?

"Does he really have a niece? Are you sure? Even if he does, I think he's just using her as an excuse."

Adam asked if she wasn't being a bit harsh on the man.

"You're the one who says I should not judge him by his past. Why are you so sure he's guilty this time?

Guilty or not, he was lying for sure. Jenny had talked to Betty Sue. Wilson hadn't stuck to her the night of the party like he said. He had been out of her sight several times.

"Now you're talking," Adam perked up. "I can confront him with this. Thanks for giving me the ammo."

They reached Seaview a few minutes later and Adam bid her goodnight. Jenny's feet were aching and she felt she was tired enough to fall asleep. Her phone beeped with a message from

Jason. As expected, he was putting up at a hotel that night. Jenny sent off an acknowledgement and went in.

Sleep did not elude her and Jenny didn't stir until her alarm went off. She made breakfast, did her deliveries and then fixed lunch. The daily routine kept her occupied well into the afternoon. Captain Charlie turned up at the café, just as she and Star were heading home.

"Hey!" she greeted. "How are you? We missed you at breakfast."

He told them he had gone to a neighboring town to meet a man about a boat.

"I'm going to be busy again, Jenny. Good thing, because I was tired of twiddling my thumbs."

Jenny was a bit relieved when she heard the Isabella was back in business. The casino was going to open that evening.

"That means I'm ferrying passengers, just as they hired me to do."

Billy arrived just then and heard Captain Charlie.

"What's that? I never even played any slots that night." He rubbed his hands with glee. "Shall we try our luck?"

Five minutes later, Jenny was agreeing to his plan. They were all going to the Isabella that evening. Captain Charlie promised he would be waiting for them at six. The troops gathered on the wharf a few minutes before that. Heather had convinced the ladies to dress up.

Jenny stood close to Jason, wearing a hot pink silk top with a scoop neck over a black velvet skirt. Molly and Heather had taken equal care with their appearance.

"You're fabulous!" Billy gave a collective compliment. "Let's go set the night on fire."

Jenny crossed her fingers and hoped there would be no mishaps while they were on board. Captain Charlie had already made several trips and was full of gossip about the people they had ferried.

"You're the only locals."

There were a few couples but many of the guests had arrived in groups of six or more. From their talk, Captain Charlie gathered they had flown in from cities across the country, dazzled by reports of a floating Vegas. The Lombardis had swept them up in posh limousines. They were spending a couple of nights on the ship. Fun and frolic was the theme.

"They even get cash to spend at the casino." he quipped. "Quite a neat trick, huh? Kinda like using a colorful fly to reel those fish in."

It was clear the Lombardi family was determined to make a success of their latest venture. Was Bianca the brains behind it, Jenny wondered. Or Primo? Or were they just acting on the orders of the old man?

It was a pleasant evening and the salty breeze flowing over the water was refreshing. Jenny cleared her mind of unpleasant thoughts and vowed to have a good time. Heather was in an upbeat mood and it was impossible not to be happy along with her.

"I'm literally the fifth wheel," Molly groaned. "Maybe I should go back with Captain Charlie."

Billy wrapped an arm around her shoulder and assured her she was very much wanted.

"I can't handle Heather all by myself. You and Jenny can keep her in line."

That got him a punch in the arm from his formidable fiancée.

They stepped aboard on a lower deck and took the elevators up to the casino. Spanning the entire length of the ship, it offered something for everyone, right from slots to blackjack tables with ten dollar buy ins. There was a private room with a few poker tables. A seven foot tall and wide man stood outside.

"High rollers only," Jason murmured in Jenny's ear. "Not for us ordinary folks."

Not much into gambling, Jenny watched while Heather and Billy played some blackjack and spun the dice at the roulette wheel.

"I'm bored!" Heather declared ten minutes later. "And hungry. Are we going to the Steakhouse for dinner tonight?"

The dealer overheard and asked if they weren't dining at the restaurant.

"It's up one floor, in the grand ball room where the party was?"

Jenny didn't think much at first and followed the rest upstairs. They were seated at a table in the center of the room. Billy ordered champagne, playing the magnanimous host as usual. Oysters on the shell followed with prawn and white fish ceviche.

One of the servers brought a skillfully plated dish served on spoons. It was sea urchin in a green broth, dotted with chili oil.

"Amuse bouche!" He announced with a flourish. "With the chef's compliments."

Jenny picked up the spoon and ate it in a single bite.

"Oh!" she exclaimed.

"Something wrong?" the young man's face clouded. "Let me get the chef."

"No, no." Jenny held up a hand. "This is delicious. I just realized something."

Jason caught her eye. He knew what she was thinking. Were they all aware she had been fired from her job? Dario had taken her on as a consultant to curate the menu for the party. According to their agreement, she was supposed to do the same for the on board restaurant later. Nobody had informed her the restaurant was open again. The menu handed to them had none of her dishes.

The server stood there, looking embarrassed. Jenny took the plunge and asked the question uppermost in her mind.

"What happened to the menu I worked on?" She paused. "You do remember who I am?"

He nodded vigorously.

"Of course, Miss Jenny." He stepped closer and leaned toward her. "Primo's taken over the restaurant now. There's going to be the main menu and a local menu. That old guy, Mr. Campbell, is going to be in charge of that."

Jenny was mortified. She tried to stay calm and pasted a smile on her face.

"The Steakhouse is Pelican Cove's best restaurant. They will make you proud."

The boy finally left, promising to check on their order.

Jenny pushed her chair back and stood up. Jason flung his napkin on the table and followed.

"Stay. I just need some fresh air. It's a bit stuffy in here."

"Don't take this hard, honey." He took her hand. "It's just a job."

Jenny whirled around and headed to the closest exit sign. She heard footsteps behind her and guessed Molly or Heather were on her tail. All she could think about was going out on an open deck to take some deep breaths of the fresh sea air.

The door swung open and deposited her in a closed passage. She walked down it and realized she had entered a veritable maze. The passage was like an artery, branching off into different directions. Based on the numbers pasted, they led to guest cabins. Did any of them end in a deck? Jenny decided to keep going straight until the passage curved. She ran smack dab into a girl who was coming out of a cabin.

"I'm sorry!" she blurted and looked up, staring at the girl from the spring festival.

Chapter 19

"You!" Jenny exclaimed. "Just the person I was looking for."

The girl's face was blank.

"Did you want any drinks? One of the guys promised to mind the bar for me."

It was Jenny's turn to be confused. Introducing herself as Katie, the girl explained she was a bartender. She thought they needed a cocktail.

"Yes, yes. Everyone at the party was talking about the drinks you mixed. You must be quite experienced."

Katie looked pleased. She told them she had worked for a cruise line for a few years and had been trained by big names in the profession.

"I took this job to be close to family. And it pays really well."

Did it pay well enough to risk her life, Jenny almost blurted. But she held herself back.

"I think I saw you at the spring festival," she forged ahead. "You were talking to Dario's body guard."

"So what?"

"Can you tell me what you're hiding? What is it that you wanted to tell someone?"

Katie clammed up. She had to get back to her job. Jenny forced her to answer one last question.

"Did you see Dario leave the party? Do you have any idea where he went? I'm trying to trace his movements." She took a deep breath. "This will stay between us, I promise."

Katie hesitated. Then she jerked a thumb over her shoulder. "He went out."

She stalked past them without another word, before Jenny had a chance to consider what she'd said.

"Did she mean he went into a cabin?" Heather asked.

They walked farther down the passage and came to a door. There was a red sign proclaiming it as an exit. Jenny pushed it open and finally stepped out into the fresh air she had been yearning for.

"A deck!" Heather exclaimed. "He came here? Why?"

They looked around. It was a semicircular space, not very large but enough for three or four people to stand about. Judging by a couple of cigarette butts littering the floor, Jenny guessed the crew came out there to smoke.

Jenny placed her hands on the sturdy railing and looked around. She could see the frothy wake of the boat and surmised they were standing at the aft. The sky was a clear inky black, studded with millions of stars.

"You think many passengers know about this?" Heather voiced her thoughts.

"Probably not." Jenny looked around. "This is very basic. Not gussied up like the guest areas of the ship."

Waves lapped against the hull in a soothing rhythm. Jenny leaned against the wall and closed her eyes, enjoying the calm. Heather sensed her mood and stood at the railing, quiet for a change. Several minutes passed before Jenny opened her eyes, ready to go back. Jason would be worried.

Her eyes landed on a trashcan in a corner. Something glinted beside it. Curious, Jenny stooped, peering at a tiny piece of metal wedged between the can and the wall. She leaned forward to pick it up.

"Wait!" Heather tapped her shoulder and handed her a tissue. "Use this. It may have fingerprints."

"Good thinking." Jenny praised.

Very carefully, she covered the object with the tissue and picked it up. She opened her palm and the two friends stared at the piece of gold resting on the white surface.

"It's a cufflink."

"I think it's embossed," Jenny muttered. "But it's too dark here to tell."

They went back into the passage and walked until they came to an overhead light. Jenny opened her palm and gazed at the cufflink.

"I was right. See those initials?"

She could see a letter W. There was one more letter but it was obscured by a dark brown substance.

"Do you think ..." she sucked in a breath.

Heather scrunched her face up in a grimace and stepped back.

"It could be anything."

They agreed it was time to head back to their table. It took them a long time to go to the main deck where the restaurant was. Billy and Jason were both looking tense.

"We're back!" Heather said cheerfully. "Did you miss us?"

Billy collapsed in obvious relief. Jason's frown deepened.

"What took you so long, Jenny? You gave me a couple of gray hair."

She apologized and gave her husband a certain look. He gave a nod, saying nothing when she sat and transferred the contents of her fist to her handbag.

"Heather and I had some unexpected luck. I have a feeling about this."

Billy had followed the silent exchange between husband and wife. He also noted Heather's barely concealed excitement.

"You may be jumping to conclusions," he warned. "There are hundreds of people on this ship. Whatever you found might belong to anyone."

Jenny thanked him but refused to lose hope. She really believed she had found a valuable piece of evidence.

"I'm sure those initials belong to a certain Senator we are familiar with. One who was on the Isabella." She sighed. "And that dirty stuff it's caked in ..." she dropped her voice to a whisper. "It could be blood."

The police would be able to run some tests on it and check if it belonged to Dario.

Pleased that their sojourn to the Isabella had proved fruitful, Jenny turned her attention to the food. They were enjoying a spectacular presentation of Baked Alaska when she spotted Primo across the room. He was schmoozing a group of men who were rich land owners from the South, judging by their bolo ties, large hats and expensively clad wives. Without a second thought, she raised her hand and waved.

His brows came together for a split second before he assumed a benign expression and waved back. Jenny kept watching him while savoring her dessert. Primo stood chatting with the group for a few minutes, glancing her way a couple of times. He shook hands with the men and strode to their table.

"Welcome to the Isabella!" he greeted. "Are you folks having a good time? How was everything?"

Billy praised the wagyu steak he had eaten. Heather told him the lobster thermidor had been the best she had ever tried. Jenny went in for the kill.

"Did I miss your message about the restaurant being open?" She smiled. "I thought we had an agreement?"

Primo was openly antagonistic but he did his best to mask his feelings.

"Dario shouldn't have raised your hopes. There is no need to hire a local nobody when we have the best chefs in the world working for us."

Jenny agreed. She had just curated the menu, providing insight into what the locals and visitors to Pelican Cove expected. It had been an extra step to ensure the Isabella was successful.

"I guess you'll wind everything up, now that Dario's gone. Are you going to sell the Isabella?"

"Not a chance!" he erupted. "Who told you that?"

Hadn't he believed the casino was a bad idea? If it wasn't making money, what was the point in keeping it going?

Primo's eyes hardened. He placed his hands on the table and leaned forward.

"Look lady. There's nothing wrong with the idea of this business. A casino on a luxury ship with the best global cuisine? The rich and famous are lining up to spend a couple of nights on the Isabella." He sneered. "Dario was the one I had a problem with. Kid had never done a day's work in his life. Had no idea what he was doing."

Jenny pressed her advantage.

"Is that what you and Bianca were discussing that night?"

Primo gave a loud snort. Jenny had broken through any walls of caution he had erected. There was no hint of evasion in his response.

"Are you high? I never talked to Bianca at the party. She was sulking anyway, after that big fight she had with Dario."

"Oh?" Jenny gave him the slightest nudge.

"It was right before the toast," Primo rambled. "Little bro' was supposed to give it, seeing as how the Isabella is his baby. But Bianca had to go and poke the bear. Dario flew into a temper. Told her to get off the boat that instant."

Primo told them that Dario was confident the Isabella would be a big success. He was already thinking ahead, planning to expand, create a fleet of such casinos on fancy ships. Bianca scoffed at the idea and told him he was immature. They argued like cat and mouse and Dario finally told her he wanted her to get lost. He didn't want her near any of his ventures.

A hush fell over the table as they all digested this. Primo stopped, finally running out of steam. He was breathing heavily, as if he had just run a mile.

Jenny was seething inside, thinking how easily Bianca had lied to her. But she tried to stay calm.

"That's a lot of drama. I must congratulate you for holding everything together." She smiled. "The oldest sibling bears the brunt of it, every time."

Mollified by the compliment, Primo bid them good night and told them to forget about getting the check.

"Compliments of the Isabella. I hope you tell your friends you had a good time. And come again!"

They stared at each other after the scion of the Lombardi family left. Billy cleared his throat.

"How about more champagne? Since that ape's footing the bill anyway?"

Jason shook his head and stood up. He took Jenny's wrap from the back of her chair and placed it on her shoulders.

"Let's go."

Captain Charlie arrived five minutes after they reached the lower deck where they had boarded. Soon, they were speeding over a calm ocean, heading toward shore. Jenny was exhausted but her mind was spinning hundred miles an hour.

They parted at the pier and Jenny went home with Jason.

"You're a marvel," he told her on the way back. "But watch your back, honey."

Jenny made a solemn promise. She was exhausted and sleep overcame her the moment they entered the house.

"Good night!" With a deep yawn, she flung off her dress, slipped on a robe and collapsed on the bed.

Morning came soon enough. Star made breakfast while Jenny drank a large mug of coffee, her eyes half closed.

"I'm tired of doing these deliveries."

"You've earned a lot of goodwill because of them, sweetheart. All these darlings are so grateful."

They set off after a quick meal of eggs and toast. Jenny finally got a chance to sit after she had served every person waiting at the café.

"Why don't you go home and rest a bit?" Star suggested. "Looks like you had a wild time on that boat last night."

Hearing about the Isabella jolted Jenny out of her stupor.

"No, no. I have to go talk to Adam. It's urgent!"

She walked to the police station on auto pilot, unable to stop yawning. Adam was standing on the steps and spotted her.

"Hey Jenny! What brings you here so early?"

They went into his office and she responded with a quick nod when he offered her coffee. Rummaging in her bag, she pulled out the tissue wrapped cufflink.

"Guess where I found this."

Adam pulled on a pair of gloves and picked up the cufflink. His eyes sparkled with excitement.

"My men searched the Isabella from bow to stern."

"Apparently not. They clearly missed this."

She pointed out the initials, especially the W.

"My money's on Senator Worth. Do you think you can analyze that stuff? Looks like dried blood to me."

Her eyes gleamed in triumph as they met Adam's. What if the blood belonged to Dario? They would be able to pin the murder on the Senator.

"This is the first concrete piece of evidence we have found." He gave her a high five. "Thank you for bringing this in, Jenny."

Chapter 20

Jenny tried to give herself a pep talk as she walked back to the café. Surely the police would be able to make something of the cufflink? If the Senator was involved, he needed to answer their questions. But he had enough power and money to bend laws.

The foreman was waiting for her when she reached the Boardwalk Café.

"This is your lucky day," he beamed. "We are ready to give you a walkthrough."

Jenny couldn't believe what she was hearing.

"This is a bit abrupt. You gave me no indication you were close to being done."

Hadn't he been saying that for a week?

"Week? You have said that for the past month."

"No harm done." He smiled. "Shall we begin?"

Jenny shook her head. This was a big moment. She wanted her friends and family with her when she got the first look.

And they could all give their feedback at once. The foreman looked disappointed but he agreed.

"Tomorrow morning at ten. We'll do some cleaning and polishing until then and have everything ship shape."

She gave an approving nod and sat down, glad to get off her feet. Her stomach gave a growl and she realized she hadn't eaten anything. There was a box of muffins on the side table. A sudden craving for a fluffy omelet stuffed with peppers, mushrooms and bacon, oozing with cheese overcame her. Maybe in a day or two, she consoled herself. It would take some time to get up to speed in the new kitchen.

"What are you smiling about?" Heather's voice intruded her thoughts.

She came up the steps, a knitting bag slung over her shoulder, holding a Tupperware container. Betty Sue was close behind, more harried than usual.

"Fancy a frittata?" Heather offered.

Jenny almost snatched the box from her and flung open the lid.

"Not the omelet I was craving but I'll take it."

Heather handed her a fork.

"You've been busy this morning."

Jenny didn't bother asking how she knew. No doubt someone had seen her at the police station and tattled. She took a few quick bites, surprised at how tasty it was.

"Did you make this?"

"Fat chance." Heather jerked a thumb toward Betty Sue. "But Grandma's getting tired of having to cook."

Other than a roll of her eyes, there was no response from Betty Sue. She cracked a smile when Jenny mentioned the grand reveal scheduled for the next day.

"I want everyone here. We'll go in together."

Star had come out, brushing a strand of hair from her face.

"Petunia would be proud of you, sweetie."

Molly joined them and was brought up to speed. Heather had taken the initiative to fix their coffee and warm the muffins.

"Are you not feeling well this morning?" Jenny picked a walnut out of her muffin and asked Betty Sue. "I hope you have not missed any doctor's appointment."

"Billy takes care of that now." Betty Sue sighed. "He reminds me of my son."

She poured out the latest drama unfolding in town. There had been more mischief at the spring festival.

"Nothing wrong with my cannolis, I hope?" Jenny cried.

Betty Sue held up her hand. It had been a minor incident. Someone had dumped a lot of salt in the food. People had gagged and almost thrown up.

This is what started a rumor about the food from the trucks being unpalatable.

The locals had been quick to blame the food truck owners. They in turn had accused the local stall owners of tampering with their food.

"What?" Jenny was astounded. "That's going too far. They are ready to make people sick just to prove a point?"

Heather agreed with her. The locals were not happy about the short circuit and the resulting fire. This was their way of getting back.

Star asked what the festival committee was doing to handle the situation.

"You need to take strict action, Betty Sue. The people of Pelican Cove have never acted like this before. Whether it is the locals or the outsiders who are causing these problems, heads need to roll."

The local stall owners had been levied a hefty fine. That had caused a further outrage. They protested that nobody had said a word to the food truck owners for causing the short circuit.

Jenny couldn't help feeling bewildered. She had a strong hunch the situation was more complicated. The best course of action was to cancel the festival. But the spring festival was a matter of pride for the town.

Her thoughts were interrupted by a shadow looming over her. She jerked her head and looked into a pair of light brown eyes that were colder than the weather.

"Quinn!" she spat. "What brings you here?"

"Can we talk?"

Jenny went down the café steps to the boardwalk, giving him no choice but to follow. She didn't want the others within hearing distance. The man had probably brought a message from the Lombardis. She fully expected some threats.

Quinn overtook her a few yards away from the café and turned around to face her.

"Whoa!"

Jenny folded her arms and stared back, defiant.

"No need to get so riled up. I have some information that might help."

"Enlighten me."

Quinn believed he had found something critical. The man had been going over all the security footage captured on the ship. One of the men had thought they saw a familiar face but couldn't place it.

"We scoured through tapes from the family's other properties."

They had not had much luck but in the process, the man realized he recognized the face from several years ago. That had prompted them to look at old tapes. Since they did not have access to those on the ship, Quinn and the man had gone up to New Jersey to a warehouse that housed older stuff from various places.

"And?" Jenny smirked. "Are you going somewhere with this?"

Quinn's response matched hers. He had hit pay dirt.

"The man was caught counting cards at our old casino in Atlantic City. Dario called him out and they had a fight. Security had thrown the man out, warning him to never come back."

Jenny asked if he had a photo.

"I went ahead and figured out who he is. Goes by the name Peter Wilson. Runs a garage here, apparently."

"No way!" Jenny couldn't hide her shock. "And you think Wilson was on the Isabella for the same purpose? To cheat at blackjack?"

Quinn shook his head. What if Wilson had come to settle a score?

"The Lombardis are not to be messed with. When Dario caught that guy all those years ago, I'm sure he spread the word. That would mean this guy was persona non grata in every casino in Atlantic City."

"So?" Jenny gave a shrug.

"He was stripped of his livelihood," Quinn explained. "Clearly, he had to flee the region and settle for this two pony town. Must have rankled."

Peter Wilson was a family man, Jenny argued. He had a flourishing business and was doing well. What's more, he was known to be a hard worker.

"I don't think being kicked out of that casino was his loss. He may have found a new lease on life."

That didn't mean anything, Quinn insisted. What if Wilson had a score to settle? He must have come to the Isabella to confront Dario.

"And kill him?" Jenny was astounded. "That's farfetched. It doesn't sound real."

Quinn gave a sigh.

"Reality can sometimes be stranger than the movies."

Jenny tried to imagine what might have happened. Had Wilson asked Dario to meet him on a deserted deck? He might have just intended to punch the man to settle a score but he hit too hard and Dario fell into the water. Wilson panicked and fled from the spot.

"What do you want me to do?"

"Tell the Sheriff, of course." Quinn hooked his thumbs in the pockets of his chinos. "They can question the guy."

Too dazed to ask more questions, Jenny gave him a nod. Giving her a mock salute, Quinn walked away.

"What was that?" Heather pounced as soon as Jenny climbed up to the deck. "Isn't that the PI who works for them?" She pointed at the Isabella in the distance.

They listened with wide eyes as Jenny narrated what Quinn had said.

"Wilson a murderer?" Heather exclaimed. "Impossible!"

Jenny wasn't that sure. They knew he had a criminal past. It was very likely he had killed before.

"But he's changed," Star argued. "He's devoted to his wife and kids. I don't think Peter will do anything to endanger the life he's built here."

Betty Sue didn't have an opinion but her eyes had narrowed in thought.

Molly thought Star had hit the nail on the head. They all agreed Wilson's family meant everything to him. But what if that was threatened?

"Think about it. Dario's been in and out of town for the past few weeks. It was only a matter of time before he ran into Wilson."

Jenny didn't see what the problem was. Several years had passed since the incident Quinn reported.

"Over twenty years, considering how long Wilson's been married. The chance of Dario recognizing him was slim."

"The stakes were too high," Molly persisted. "What if Wilson decided he didn't want to risk it? So he struck first."

Chapter 21

Heather convinced Jenny to go to the spring festival. The lunch hour was approaching and it was another chance to eat the exotic food offered by the outsiders.

"That's not why you want to go there," Jenny teased. "Admit it."

"Okay, okay. So I love a good scandal. What's wrong with getting a piece of the action, checking things out?"

Star was worried about their wellbeing. If the food had been tampered with, was it safe to eat? Betty Sue agreed with her and forbid them from taking a single bite.

"Come on, Grandma!" Heather stood her ground. "Either shut the festival down or get on board."

Betty Sue gave up and went back to the inn, Star in tow. They were going to heat up a can of soup.

The two younger women set off at a brisk pace for the festival grounds.

"Would you look at that?" Jenny exclaimed.

Throngs of people occupied the area. There was a line at the ticket booth. All the tables set up under a marquee were full of people digging into mounds of food. And the trucks were doing brisk business.

"Glad we came, huh?" Heather quipped.

Was the whole drama around food just a rumor then? Jenny stalked to an area where the members of the festival committee sat, keeping an eye on the crowd. Barb Norton was playing with the strand of pearls around her neck, bobbing her head as she listened to Ada Newbury complain about something.

"What's going on here?" Jenny burst out. "That whole bunkum about the food being bad …"

Barb told her they had taken care of it. The food truck owners had thrown out everything they had stored or prepped in advance. They submitted to a strict inspection by the festival committee.

"We made sure all the surfaces were scrubbed clean and there wasn't a single item in their store."

One of the volunteers had been present at every truck when the food was prepared. And the Sheriff had provided extra security.

"No adverse incident today," Barb reported.

"How many items have you tasted yourself?" Heather needled, giving a dry laugh when Barb flushed. "What about you, Aunt Ada?"

The two women glared at them.

Jenny pulled at Heather's arm and forced her to walk away.

"Let's find out one way or the other."

They headed to the taco truck and ordered fish tacos and churros. They looked around for a place to sit. Luckily, a boy and a girl were getting up from the table.

"Let's go!" Heather rushed ahead.

"Hey! We know that girl."

Jenny stared at the bartender from the ship. What was her name? Katie?

The girl's eyes were red and streaks of mascara stained her face. It was obvious she had been crying.

"Is the food that bad?" Jenny joked. "Or too spicy?"

The boy with her bristled with barely suppressed anger. Jenny noted it wasn't Dario's bodyguard.

"That scoundrel didn't treat her well," he burst out. "But at least he's dead. Be happy you got off easy."

Jenny offered her churros to the girl. She hesitated, then picked up the hot fluffy pastry and dunked it in the pot of melted chocolate. Deciding to give her time, Jenny bit into a taco.

"This is yum!" Heather gave her a high five. "We should bring some for Star and Grandma."

Just when Jenny thought the silence around the table was getting uncomfortable, the boy exploded.

"That rascal wound Katie around his little finger. Poor thing actually believed he loved her. I told her he was a famous playboy." He nudged an elbow in the girl's side. "Didn't I show you that fancy magazine? Guy was photographed naked with that famous pop star."

A fresh spurt of tears started flowing down the girl's eyes. Jenny caught the boy's eye and gave him a stare, silently warning him to be quiet.

She pulled a tissue out of her bag and handed it to the bartender.

"It's hard to lose someone you love. Even when it's one sided and your feelings are not returned."

"He was wrong for me," the girl sobbed. "But he s-said he was falling in love with me." She blew her nose in the soggy tissue. "And I believed him."

Jenny could feel Heather give a mental eye roll.

"Maybe he was serious about you." Jenny offered her some hope. "Dario had grand plans for the Isabella and he once told me he was very impressed by the Eastern Shore." She crossed her fingers behind her back. "I think he meant you."

The girl sat up straighter and picked up another churro. She ate it really quickly, making Jenny wonder how long the poor child had been starving herself.

"In any case, he didn't deserve to be killed in that brutal manner. I am doing what I can to catch the culprit." Jenny sucked in a breath. "It's nice to know someone on that ship cared about him."

The boy gave a snort and looked away. They all ignored him.

"Can I come to you if I have any questions?"

The girl nodded.

"And if you remember anything, no matter how silly, promise you will come and tell me, hon. Don't sit on it."

She locked eyes on the girl, encouraging her to open up. Surprisingly, it was the boy who spoke.

"I kinda heard something." He began. "That scoundrel ..."

"You mean Dario?" Jenny interrupted him.

"Yeah, yeah. Boss Man. Or dead man, I should say." He sniggered. "Dead man had a screaming match with another guy."

Jenny was beginning to lose track of the number of people Dario had been in arguments with. She asked the boy what he did on the ship. Turned out he was a waiter in the restaurant but also acted as a cabin steward when required.

"This other guy told the boss his business was going under pretty soon." He frowned, trying to remember more. "They went back and forth and were at each others' throats."

He had hovered beside them, holding a tray of drinks he was taking to the ball room.

"That guy suddenly pulled a card out of his pocket and flung it at me. Told me I was gonna be out of a job soon. I could go to him when that happened."

He reached into the pocket of his grubby jeans and came up with a wrinkled business card. Jenny took it from him and asked where all this had happened.

"In a passage off the ball room, where that party was. I think they were just getting ready for the toast."

Jenny finally darted a look at the card she was holding. Her eyes widened in shock when she saw the name embossed in gold print. Antonio Bellini. Petunia's cousin.

Her mind began to race with different theories. The bartender was looking much better and Jenny stood up.

"I'm getting more churros. Do you want anything, Heather?"

She wanted to check out the lamb sliders a cart was offering.

"Thank you Ma'am," the girl blubbered. "You're very kind."

"Remember what I said," Jenny stressed. "Let me know if you need anything."

She walked away and headed to the trucks, Heather in tow.

"That was quite an exit. What's on that card?"

Jenny showed it to her. Heather gave a low whistle. Were the Bellinis part of the whole mess after all?

"Tony was here. We know that. All that nonsense about wanting to visit Petunia was just a pack of lies."

The Senator had told them the Bellinis were very interested in setting up a casino on the shore. But Dario Lombardi had somehow beaten them to it.

"You think this Tony was the guy with the burner phone?" Heather was ahead of her. "He must have arranged to meet Dario."

They evaluated the reasons why he might do that. Jenny didn't know much about these people. It was obvious they were business rivals. Were they on talking terms with each other? Maybe they had grown up in the same area and had known each other since childhood. They could even have common relations or friends.

"Tony was taunting him." Jenny mused as they stopped before the burger truck.

Heather placed an order for the lamb sliders and curly fries.

"If he intended to murder the man, why would he get into an argument with him in a public place?" She looked at the card again. "And this is clear proof he was on the ship. He wouldn't flaunt this."

Heather collected their food and they walked back to the marquee.

"It might have been an accident. So this guy Tony mocks Dario and goes off. Dario works himself up in a lather and shoots off a message to meet on that deck."

To what purpose, Jenny questioned.

"Just give him a piece of his mind, maybe." Heather shrugged. "They have a shouting match again and this time things take a turn for the worse."

The squabble turned violent and physical and they pushed each other around.

"You mean it was an accident?"

It was a theory worth exploring, Jenny thought.

"He lied about going to the ship. Tony said he never set foot on the Isabella."

Heather told her to take a break from all the speculation. Jenny realized she had hardly eaten a thing. She picked up a slider and dipped it into the extra sauce.

"This is nice! Mint and cucumber in yogurt. And there's some spice. Cumin, I think."

They both licked sauce off their fingers, agreeing the food was delicious. All the rumors about the food from the trucks being bad sounded fake.

"I think we should give credit where it's due."

Heather tipped her head in the direction of the trucks. Barb Norton stood beside the Thai truck, eating chicken satay. Ada Newbury ate salad from a fried taco shell.

"Shall we get one of those skewers?" Jenny beamed, glad to see some of the older locals beginning to walk toward the trucks. "The tide may be turning and we better grab some before they run out."

"Miss Jenny!" A cheery voice interrupted. "Hey Miss Jenny!" Another chirped.

She found herself wrapped into a tangle of arms from both sides. They smelt like freshly mowed grass with a hint of honeysuckle.

"Evie, Rosie!! How are you, sweethearts? When did you get into town?"

Jenny had a lot of affection for Adam's twin daughters. She had almost become their stepmom. Luckily, the status of her relationship with their father had never come between them.

"We flew in last night." Rosie gushed. "Evie's back from Kuwait. We took pity on poor Dad."

One of the twins had followed in her father's footsteps and enlisted in the army. She had already distinguished herself in an operation and been recommended for a medal.

"It's good to have you home safe." Jenny hugged them again. "Adam's so proud of you. We all are!"

They asked after her son.

"He better come and visit." Rosie flung her mane of glossy blonde hair over her shoulder and finally noticed Heather. "Hey! Have you set a date yet?"

"I was beginning to feel invisible." Heather frowned, then smiled, opening her arms wide. "Come and gimme a hug, you brutes!"

The twins spoke in tandem, bubbling with enthusiasm. Jenny found it catching.

"What's this about a casino offshore?" Evie asked, picking up a bunch of fries from Jenny's plate and dunking them in the tub of ketchup. "We're dying to go check it out."

Chapter 22

Jenny had a spring in her step the next morning. After months of enduring the several inconveniences of having builders in the café, she was finally going to see what they had achieved. She wore a floral pink dress as a nod to spring, took special care with her makeup and rushed through the deliveries.

The line of people waiting at the café were equally excited.

"When does the café open?" Captain Charlie asked. "That's all these folks are yapping about."

Jenny held up her hand and gathered everyone around her. She thanked them for being patient.

"I know this has been very inconvenient for all of you. But I beg you to bear this for a few more days."

Weren't the men done with their work, a woman asked.

"I'm getting the walkthrough today. There may ... may be a few more changes. Hopefully, everything will be perfect. We need to set up the new furniture after that, do some trial runs in the kitchen." She smiled. "And then we'll have a grand reopening party."

A cheer went up in the crowd.

"Everyone's invited."

The foreman and his crew were busy doing some last minute cleaning inside. He had promised Jenny it would all be shinier than a new penny.

She was glad when the customers began to leave. Captain Charlie remained. Jenny spotted Jason on the boardwalk and rushed to meet him.

"You came!" She let herself be wrapped in a tight hug.

"Of course." Jason laughed, giving her a quick kiss on the cheek. "No way I'm going to miss this, hon. It's going to be great."

The Magnolias began to arrive. Star and Betty Sue walked together. Billy and Heather followed them. Molly came last, holding a large folder.

Jenny welcomed everyone and they stood about, waiting for the summons. The foreman came out and looked around. He rubbed his hands and grinned.

"Don't you prefer to come in through the main door?"

A ripple of laughter traveled through the group and they went around the café to the front entrance. Jenny was surprised to see a fat red ribbon tied across the door. A red carpet was slung over the steps. One of the crew came forth with a tray holding a pair of scissors. Jason began to clap and everyone joined in.

Jenny teared up. If only Petunia had been with them to share this moment.

She took her aunt's arm and placed the scissors in her hand.

"You do the honors."

Star's eyes were moist. She protested with all her might.

"This is your baby, Jenny. Thanks to you, the Boardwalk Café is famous up and down the coast. You've given new life to the place and the town."

Jenny shook her head.

"I couldn't have done it without you, though. You took me in when I was foundering. I was a ship without a rudder." She opened her arms wide and gathered all her friends together. "You all saved my life and I'm so grateful. I don't say it enough but I love you."

That set everyone off. Billy sported a helpless look. Captain Charlie had a broad smile pasted on his face. Jason cleared his throat and sought their attention.

"Why don't we go in? There will be enough time for speeches later."

Finally, Star cut the ribbon and Jenny pushed the doors open.

The smell of fresh paint invaded her senses. She stepped in and turned around in a circle, her mouth open in awe. Her wide eyes took in every single detail.

"This is ... this is the exact shade of blue I wanted."

The foreman chuckled. "It's the same one you chose, Missy."

The furniture was polished, upholstered in the blue and white striped fabric Jenny and Molly had chosen. One wall was hung with black and white pictures depicting the town's history. And the greatest attraction of all was the grand mural Star had painted.

"Wow!" Jenny exclaimed. "This is beyond anything I imagined. So beautiful."

Heather had moved to a small room off the main dining room. It had been a coat closet earlier but had been locked for several years. They had come up with the idea of turning it into a gallery for Star's paintings.

Jenny admired the canvases adorning the walls. They depicted different landscapes across the island - sunrises, sunsets, marshes, various seasons. Framed in gilt and hung on glossy white walls, they certainly stood out.

The foreman urged her to step into the kitchen. Jenny followed him, pulse racing. The kitchen was the heart of the café. She went in and was immediately struck by the vista of the ocean stretching before her. Speechless, she stared ahead, unable to believe her eyes.

"This was part of the design," the foreman joked. "Don't you like the window?"

The spanking new stainless appliances and the industry standard refrigerator paled in comparison to the natural light bathing the kitchen. The countertops gleamed and the new sink had no cracks in it.

"I think I can work with this." Jenny said and burst into tears.

It was a morning to remember. Half an hour later, they all sat in the dining room, sipping cappuccinos. Heather had taken on the mighty industry grade coffee machine Jenny had invested in and turned out some respectable cups.

"We need to hire a barista."

"No need." Heather took it as an affront. "I'm a bit rusty but I can get up to speed once we get the full demo the company has offered. Set it up soon, Jenny."

None of them had the energy to oppose Heather. Adam came in as they were moaning over the absence of cookies. He had arrived via the deck so none of them saw him enter.

"Hey Jenny!" He stood with his arms on his hips, gazing around. "You don't do anything in half measure."

Jason offered him a chair.

"Looks like I'm crashing a private party. Does this mean the café is open, Jenny?"

She waved off his protests. He was among friends.

"I'm so glad my extended family is here with me today." She beamed. "We just got a first look. I'll be getting up to speed in the kitchen. But the café should be up and running in a few days."

Heather churned out another cappuccino and handed it to Adam. He thanked her and sat with them, listening to Captain Charlie recount one of his stories.

"Can I borrow you for a minute?" He asked Jenny after he had taken a few sips.

Intrigued, she followed him out to the deck.

"The results from the cufflink came back."

"And?" Jenny held her breath.

"It's a match. It's Dario's blood alright."

Unfortunately, that did not help them much. They still needed to prove the cufflink belonged to Senator Worth. The police were trying hard.

"We need a search warrant but no judge is going to issue one just because the initials on the cufflink match his."

Jenny realized he was right. She stared at the sunlight reflecting off the sea waves and racked her brain for options.

"I noticed a lot of people were taking pictures with him. And then a photographer was clicking pictures of the whole party. Why not check them out? If one of the photos captures him wearing those links, we'll have our proof."

Adam almost hugged her in his excitement.

"That's brilliant. Why didn't I think of that?" His face fell. "Do you think I'm the stereotypical small town policeman, all bluster but no brains?"

Jenny couldn't hold back her laughter.

"Adam Hopkins! Are you fishing for compliments? You are handling dozens of cases at once. I'm sure you would've figured it out sooner or later."

He wanted to know if she had made any progress. Jenny told him about Tony Bellini.

"He's trying to prove himself, I think. Maybe old man Bellini blames him for losing the casino deal. You think he murdered Dario just to impress his family?"

Adam said they couldn't rule it out. He cursed the day the Lombardis had arrived in Pelican Cove. They had ushered in a level of crime the town had never seen.

"The stakes are too high. Philomena Ryder fell prey to these criminals. I just hope we capture this killer before he strikes again."

Jenny was thinking about the Senator. What motive could he have to kill Dario?

"We need some dirt on him but it's difficult. He's surrounded by toadies who are all vying for his attention. They have vested interests. None of them will say a word against him, Jenny."

What about his opponents, she wondered. He must have plenty, being in politics. There would be journalists who had conducted research on him.

"Excellent!" Adam praised. "You're on a roll today. I'll get on it right away."

He pressed his lips together and sat at a table, gazing around him. Jenny guessed he was debating something in his mind. Was it another clue related to the investigation?

"We had an anonymous tip." He finally revealed. "Dario's sister announced a reward. Quite a generous one, for anyone giving information that would help us."

Jenny leaned against her table and folded her arms, waiting to hear more.

"Dario owed a lot of money to someone. A high roller, the person calling in the tip said. That's a gambler who spends big money at the casino."

"And?"

"This man was pressuring him to pay up."

Jenny spotted the flaw in the theory right away.

"Are you saying this gambler murdered Dario because he didn't return a loan? That makes no sense. His interest lies in keeping him alive."

Adam agreed with her. But he pointed out how it was plausible. All the information they had found until now indicated Dario's death was a spur of the moment crime. Dario might have called him to beg for more time. The conversation got out of hand and he ended up dead.

Or what if the gambler had been annoyed that the Lombardis were spending so much on the big launch? He might have confronted Dario and asked for his money back.

It was something to think about. The tip had not revealed the identity of the high roller. Jenny didn't think it was legit. Someone had made up the story to lay their hands on the reward money.

"That's my gut feel too." Adam agreed with her. "Well, Jenny. I need to push off. Good job with the café."

"I'm going to need your help tasting some of the new items on the menu." She shrugged, feeling vulnerable all of a sudden. "You think the locals will approve of the new décor?"

Adam told her they would be coming in droves. Then he floored her by giving an indirect compliment.

"It's my loss, of course. You probably won't have any time left to solve murders."

Chapter 23

The blue waters of the Chesapeake Bay shimmered in the mid-day sun. Jenny sighed with pleasure, feeling a sense of relief wash over her. She had been on tenterhooks, not knowing if the renovation would be worth all the expense and trouble. Now after a first look, she was pleased and bubbling with energy.

"We need storage bins for the pantry, jars for spices and herbs, squeezy bottles for ketchup and mustard ..." she rattled off the list she had been making as Jason drove.

"Time enough for all that. Why don't we grab some lunch first? What do you fancy?"

They exited the bridge and entered the city of Virginia Beach. Jason drove to a small rustic joint on a side street that sold the best fish and chips. Jenny told him it was perfect. She didn't want to spend time over an elaborate lunch.

The white fish was fresh and the tartar sauce had the right kick. Jenny's mind was racing at the speed of light, trying to keep track of orders she needed to place, new menus, kitchen organization and so on.

"Do you think I can be ready in a week?"

"No need to rush," Jason warned. "Set up everything just as you want it. You will not be doing this again for some time."

He was right, of course. Once the tourist rush began, Jenny wouldn't have a free moment. And she hadn't even thought of the herb garden. The contractors had cleared a small patch for her and the Cohens had sent their own gardener to design the place. They had even gifted her the plants. Jenny couldn't wait for warmer weather, thrilled at the thought of plucking fresh herbs to add to her dishes. Pesto! She needed to add a pesto based sandwich to the menu. Or pasta.

"What's the frown for?" Jason asked as they climbed into the car. "Are you thinking about your dead body?"

Jenny realized she hadn't spared a single thought to the murder for the past hour.

"Actually, no. And I find that refreshing. Why do I involve myself in these things? As if I don't have enough to do."

Jason sputtered, giving way to a deep laugh.

"I don't believe you'll ever give it up, honey. You love to solve these puzzles." He glanced at her as he started the car. "Are you giving up because you've hit a wall?"

Is that what he thought? She shook her head in denial.

"I'm not a quitter, Jason Stone. You should know that by now."

Jason chuckled. He had made his point.

They drove to a warehouse retail store where Jenny was going to shop for supplies. It would take them a good forty minutes to get there.

"Let's review everything then." Jason offered.

Thankful she had such a supportive husband, Jenny began to summarize what she knew.

"Dario Lombardi was found dead on the beach, near the pier. He had been in the water for some time and he had also obviously been strangled. There is no doubt this is a murder. But what is the motive? Once we establish that, we can narrow down our suspects."

Jason wanted to go over them. Jenny agreed to do that.

"Let me warn you though. I've discussed this with Adam and the girls and gone over it in my mind several times. We're at an impasse, Jase. There is no ray of light here."

He urged her not to give up so soon.

"We'll start with Harry Campbell then." She began reluctantly, holding up her hand to ward off his protest. "Just try to be objective. I know you don't think he could do this. So do a lot of others. But we should evaluate what we know."

Jason nodded and encouraged her to continue.

"The Isabella is bad for the Steakhouse. It's going to bankrupt the business. Harry was seen fighting with Dario that night." She paused. "This is not just hearsay. We have an eye witness."

His eyes flickered. Jenny was surprised when Jason took his hand off the wheel and patted her knee.

"Not any more, I think."

With a pang, Jenny realized what he wanted to say. Philomena Ryder was dead. How could she have forgotten that? The poor woman had lost her life because she overheard a random conversation.

"Dario was a stranger but Philomena was one of us," Jason reminded her. "You have to be strong and do this for her."

Swallowing a lump, Jenny decided to move on.

"The Bellinis are in the fray, of course. We can't ignore them. I know Petunia was one of them and I owe her a lot." She expelled a breath. "I'm being ungrateful."

Jason pointed out the flaw in her thinking. Petunia had never been enamored by her family. She was so against what they did that she ran away from home and assumed a new identity. Inspite of having access to millions, she had slaved like an ordinary person and worked hard to keep the Boardwalk Café afloat.

"Not at all. In fact, you're doing exactly what she would have done herself."

"You think so?" Jenny's eyes grew moist. "I miss her so much."

They reminisced for a while, Jenny remembering how the friendly woman had insisted she stop wallowing in her grief and start pouring coffee.

"Have the Bellinis and Lombardis brought their feud to our shores?" Jason interrupted her thoughts.

Jenny gave a shrug. Maybe it was just a question of money. They were both looking for a good opportunity and then Dario had managed to win.

"Tony Bellini wants to set up a casino real bad. He was in the process of securing permits. Senator Worth said the Bellinis were applying a lot of pressure on him. Tony was ready to fill his pockets in exchange for the proper licenses and stuff."

But had he also intended to have the casino on a ship? Jenny admitted she wasn't sure. The idea of the Isabella was entirely Dario's. But once it was out there, Tony Bellini wanted to capitalize on it.

"But what's the motive here, Jenny? I'm not sure. He could just duplicate the idea, anchor his ship off somewhere else and rake in the moolah. There's no shortage of coastline in our country."

Jenny had a sudden urge to scratch her eyebrow. She flipped open the vanity mirror and smoothed her hand over her brows, checking her appearance. Was she looking frumpy? She rubbed the charms hanging around her neck on a gold chain. Her son gifted one to her every year on Mothers' Day. It had been ages since he had come to visit.

"Thinking of Nick?" Jason read her mind. "Want me to go up to the city and drag him down here?"

That brought a smile to her lips.

"He's busy on a new case. Why did my only son have to become a lawyer?"

She had scarcely noticed where they were going. Jason parked in front of a nondescript building. It was a rambling single story structure. There were no other cars in the parking lot.

"Why are we here?"

Jason got out and came around to her door. He urged her to hurry.

"I would ask you to close your eyes but I know you'll peep." He led her to the main entrance and pointed at a small sign hanging over the lintel.

Jenny screamed, unable to believe her eyes.

"Are we really here?"

Jason responded by taking her hand and pulling her inside. They were at the factory store of a renowned tableware company. Jenny felt like she was in Wonderland. Rows of fine china and porcelain stretched in every direction.

"We can't use those old plates now that we spruced up the whole café. This is my contribution."

Jenny thought it was the perfect gift. But it was going to be hard to choose. An hour later, they had placed an order for a few dozen plates, bowls, glasses and silverware.

"Thank you so much." Jenny was floating on thin air. "This is the best surprise ever!"

Jason smiled as he ushered her back to the car. They decided to stop for ice cream. Jenny resumed their conversation after she had taken a few large bites of her blueberry cheesecake ice cream.

"Delicious!"

Jason had gone for pineapple with toasted coconut. He said it was like a pina colada.

"I'm not very fond of Bianca Lombardi," Jenny confessed. "She's obnoxious. Likes to project that she's this powerful woman entrepreneur but we know the kind of business she's involved in."

"Most of it is legit." Jason told her he had asked an assistant to do some research. "Who knows, maybe she has the brains in the family."

"Brains, brawn and beauty!" Jenny admitted reluctantly. "Adam told me she announced a big prize for anyone giving information that would help the police." She clucked. "That makes her a saint, I guess."

Jason again wanted to know if the siblings had got along. Every such equation had an element of rivalry.

"Dario was the runt of the litter. I think he's been a wastrel most of his life. But he was really committed to this project." Jenny paused to reflect. "But his brother Primo has taken up the reins the moment he's out of the picture."

She had a hunch the old man was playing his kids against each other. It may have been a healthy contest. Or maybe he was depraved enough to have fun at their expense.

"He's the head of the family though." Jason pointed out. "I've found out that much."

They moved on to Peter Wilson. Jason believed he was the most likely candidate.

"I've always thought there was something fake about him, Jenny. This was before we knew about his past and his connection to the Bellini family. Sure, the man acts like a friendly teddy bear but he's capable of flipping in an instant."

"Are you saying he's violent?" Jenny was aghast, trying to reconcile Jason's impression with the man she liked.

"He can be," Jason quipped. "And I'm sure he has been so in the past. But I'm not clear what motive he might have here."

Jenny told him how Peter had been caught counting cards several years ago. Dario had been instrumental in cutting off his livelihood.

Had he nursed a grudge for decades and finally taken his revenge? Jason echoed what Jenny had considered herself.

"Peter is a family man. It's more likely he felt endangered and he struck first."

She was worried about the burner phone. Molly had seen Peter buy one and he had not denied it, although he gave the slim story about buying it for his niece.

"He's the only one we can tie to a disposable phone, as of now. It could be farfetched but that's all we have."

Jason had turned pale.

"Have you warned Molly to be careful?"

"You don't think ..."

"If you believe Peter got Dario out of the way, he won't stop now. He will eliminate anyone who stands in his way."

Jenny placed a call to her friend, beseeching her to watch her back. Molly just laughed.

"She thinks I'm being silly. We'll have to do it ourselves. You think I should ask Adam for help?"

Jason thought it wouldn't hurt.

"What about our illustrious Senator? He has plenty of money and power at his fingertips. That's a dangerous combination."

Jenny agreed with him but pointed out the absence of a motive.

"Adam's taking a deeper look at him. Maybe there are skeletons in his closet that led him to do this."

Jason ate the last bit of pineapple from his cup and licked his spoon.

"You need a breakthrough, Jenny. And it will happen today or in a month. You have no choice but to sit tight and wait."

Chapter 24

For the next two days, Jenny followed Jason's advice. She immersed herself into getting the café in shape. The deck furniture arrived and Heather and Molly assisted her in arranging it just so, making sure the cushion covers were on correctly. Betty Sue and Star watched them with an indulgent eye, providing their opinion when asked.

The kitchen proved to be a challenge. Jenny found it hard to navigate the new layout. She kept bumping into the center island and the countertops. And she spent most of her time staring out of the new window at the beach. The supplies arrived one by one and they stocked the pantry, arguing over the best place for everything. Jenny arranged new spatulas and knives in the kitchen drawers and unpacked the new pots and pans.

"What's the first thing you're gonna cook?" Heather wanted to know. "Please don't say chicken salad."

Jenny had an idea. She wanted Star to make her six cheese lasagna. That would allow them to do a dry run of the new oven.

"Have I gone overboard?" Jenny leaned against the island and groaned. "I could've used the old pots and pans."

Molly told her they had been in service for the past thirty or more years and had been scrubbed to death. She was very excited about all the new plates Jenny had ordered at the factory.

"Did you go for a Victorian theme? Or something in blue, to match the walls?"

"Just white with a gold rim." Jenny replied, second guessing herself again. "I want the food to shine." She admitted it had been a tough call. "There were so many patterns to choose from. You should've been there."

Heather climbed up on one of the counters and called for a break.

"I could use some coffee. Give me your fanciest orders and I'll brave the machine."

There was a whirring sound as the coffee machine ground the beans before brewing them. A hiss of steam escaped the frothing device before Heather had a jar of milk ready. The girls were laughing their heads off when a stern voice interrupted.

"Hello ladies! Can I mooch some breakfast?"

It was Adam, looking a bit haggard in a crumpled shirt with the sleeves rolled up. Jenny deduced he was staying up late, trying to crack the case.

"Sorry but I haven't really started cooking here yet. We can offer you some fancy coffee though. Caramel macchiato?"

Adam played along and tasted four different creations Heather placed before him. Her attempt at creating latte art had failed miserably. And the coffee was burnt.

"This is just terrible." He laughed. "Evie is home and she is a certified barista. Maybe she can give you tips."

Jenny had forgotten all about meeting the twins.

"Are they still here? How long are they staying? Maybe they can get Nick to come here for a visit."

Adam sidestepped the question and asked if she could spare a few minutes. Jenny waved a hand at her friends.

"It's just ... they are gonna learn about it anyway."

With a roll of his clear blue eyes, Adam leaned against a counter and brought them up to speed. He had been in touch with some of his army buddies.

"One or two of them got a job in the city, working for the government."

Did he have friends at the Pentagon, Jenny teased. Why hadn't he said anything before?

"Well, they work here and there. The specifics aren't important. Thing is, I asked them to run some checks on our

Senator." He scratched the corner of his eye, noticing the big window for the first time. "I have high hopes."

He turned to Jenny with a broad grin.

"You dreamed of this. Looking out at the ocean while you prepped and cooked. Must say the Cohens have done a great job."

Jenny agreed with him. The builders had understood her vision perfectly and given her what she wanted.

"What about the photos?"

Adam rubbed his eyes. They had requested everyone who attended the party to turn in any pictures they took.

"We are wading through thousands!" He sighed. "My staff is getting cross eyed trying to spot something relevant in them."

Molly immediately offered to help. Heather seconded her. Adam looked like he had been given a life line.

"I hope you're serious because I will take you up on that."

The girls promised to go to the police station after lunch. Jenny was gazing out through the window. She could see the Isabella anchored in the distance, a constant fixture.

"What about reviewing the scene of crime again?" she asked. "Have you gone and looked around the pier? Or gone aboard the Isabella?"

Adam gave a start. He had completely forgotten about that.

"I did go there, and guess what? I found a bit of blue fabric stuck to the railing on that deck."

Once again it had been in an awkward spot, caught on a protruding nail.

Jenny thought they were making progress.

"We found the cufflink on that deck. And now this scrap. Is it safe to assume that it's where Dario died? I mean he was already dead before he reached the pier."

"All conjecture at this point." Adam winced. "The medical examiner will not commit to a certain time, since the body was in cold water for a considerable period."

In short, the police were not certain exactly where Dario had been killed. Neither could they pinpoint a certain time.

Jenny thought of the reward the Lombardis had offered. Had the police received any tips? After all, there were dozens of people on board that night. Any one of them could have wandered off from the party and witnessed the crime.

"Tips are pouring in, Jenny. But most of them are useless. That's another thing that's keeping my staff occupied."

He gave them an example of the weird things people were calling in. One of the locals reported seeing a man in a dark coat walking by the pier the night of the party. He wore a hat pulled low over his face.

"Watching too many crime serials on TV," Adam dismissed.

Jenny thought it could be a promising lead.

"The nights are still cool and the wind can be harsh. But is it cold enough to need a coat?"

That's why the caller found it suspicious. It had been past midnight, a time when the beach was almost deserted.

Molly argued a lot of people had been around that night, attending the party on the ship. But those who refused to set foot on board had just gathered to watch the others.

"Might have come to watch the fireworks and then stuck around."

That was the most frustrating thing, Adam told them. Nothing was definite. Almost every supposed clue they found had multiple explanations.

"Anyhoo ... I should get going. You better haul yourself to the station in an hour." He pointed at Heather and Molly.

Jenny had been thinking about the scrap of cloth.

"Wait a minute ... all the Lombardis were dressed in blue suits that night. Dario said they wanted to stand out."

If the police confirmed that the scrap had not come from Dario's suit, that could mean it belonged to one of his family.

Adam brightened at the idea. But it would take time to ascertain all that. He had used up all his favors at the lab and would have to go through the normal channels.

He left after popping out on the deck to greet Betty Sue and Star.

"You're making lasagna." Jenny informed her aunt after he left. "We're here to help. But I want the first dish in the new kitchen to be cooked by you."

They all trooped back in the kitchen. There was a lot of gentle teasing and ribbing as they mixed all the cheeses in a bowl while Star devoted herself to making the red sauce.

The kitchen phone trilled, startling them. Jenny answered and beckoned to Betty Sue.

"It's for you."

Betty Sue said hello and began shaking her head. A deep blush appeared on her cheeks and a bead of sweat laced her lips.

"Calm down, Grandma!" Heather hung up the phone.

"Heather Morse!" Betty Sue boomed. "How dare you do that?"

Jenny handed her a glass of cold water and urged her to sit. The doctor had warned them to make sure Betty Sue didn't lose her temper. It was bad for her blood pressure.

"After all my family's done for this town," Betty Sue seethed.

Her chest heaved and it was a few minutes before they could coax the story out of her.

"The stall owners are accusing the festival committee of taking kickbacks."

Jenny doubled over with laughter.

"What? From whom?"

The locals claimed the food truckers had paid off the festival committee to look the other way. That's why they had not been penalized when the short circuit happened.

"But that's ridiculous!" Jenny exclaimed.

"Positively mad!" Heather agreed. "Grandma, have you seen the food they are selling? It's all top notch and costs a lot. But they are selling at very low prices."

They must be taking a hit so they could come back next year, Jenny reasoned.

"What we mean is, there is no way the food truck owners are making big money here. I doubt they are breaking even. Where would they get the money to pay off the likes of Barb Norton?"

Star wore a beatific smile as she stirred the sauce.

"What are you thinking?" Jenny asked.

Molly spoke before Star could reply.

"There's one way they are making bank." She stared at Star. "She knows what I mean."

Heather told her to spit it out.

Molly put her thumb and forefinger together and touched them to her lips, opening her mouth to blow air out.

"They are selling something else on the side."

"Marijuana?" Jenny was scandalized. "Did you see anyone smoking pot at the festival?"

Betty Sue was on the verge of losing her composure again. Heather thought it was very funny.

"Drugs? At the Pelican Cove Spring Festival? Come on, Molls. That's a scene out of the crime novel you had your head in yesterday. Things like that don't happen on our island."

Molly wasn't willing to back down.

"Oh really? Didn't we just have a murder? No wait, two murders?"

Chapter 25

Jenny stood in the middle of her kitchen, unable to believe herself. She pinched her arm and gave a yowl. Everything gleamed but it was a bit too antiseptic. What was a kitchen without pots bubbling over, counter tops full of diced vegetables and something baking in the oven? The lunch hour was approaching and Jenny debated what she should cook. She wanted it to be simple. But it also had to feed at least a dozen people.

Her bakery supplier had dropped off some fresh crusty bread. And there was a batch of cheese in the refrigerator.

Pesto, she thought to herself and began roasting some pine nuts.

Star came and sat on one of the snazzy new bar stools placed along the kitchen counter.

"I'm bored!"

She had spent the last few months engrossed in finishing the murals. Now that they were done, she had a lot of time on her hands.

"Put me to work, sweetie."

Had she picked out all the paintings she wanted to hang in the little gallery room, Jenny wanted to know. Star wanted a break from all that.

"You can shred the cheese, I guess."

Jenny sauteed some sun dried tomatoes in olive oil and added all the ingredients to the food processor. She had just offered the spatula to Star for a taste when a burly, bearded man peeped in.

"Hello!" She gave a cheery greeting. "Can I help you?"

He flashed a sheepish grin.

"I was hoping to get a bite to eat. But ..."

"No, you guessed that right." Jenny laughed. "We're not open yet."

He muttered something about Charlie leading him on. Something clicked in Jenny's mind.

You're Skip, aren't you? Captain Charlie's friend?"

He stepped into the kitchen, both hands deep in the pockets of his pants and beamed.

"That's right. He's always saying the Boardwalk Café is the best place for a meal in Pelican Cove."

"But we don't see you much." Jenny quizzed.

Skip told them he had been a fisherman for fifty years and had run charters along the Eastern Shore, just like Captain Charlie. He was half retied now.

"Wife passed last year. She was the best cook and I never had the need to grab a meal anywhere else." His eyes flickered. "Only daughter's moved up to Ocean City. I was with her for a few days, spending time with my grandkids."

He had sailed back into town that morning.

Jenny told him he had missed a lot.

"You talkin' 'bout them on the Isabella?" He jerked his neck toward the ship anchored on the water. "I told Charlie to stay away from them. Now look what's happened. Those thugs are at each other's throats. That casino will be shut down soon and Charlie will lose a bundle."

Did he mean the Lombardis had not paid Captain Charlie?

Skip knew nothing about that. He was talking about the new boat Captain Charlie had almost bought. He had taken out a loan, thinking it was a good investment. But what if the Lombardis left their shore?

Jenny told him they had heard him talking about the new boat but had no idea he was that serious. She narrated her own experience. Primo had fired her and upset all her projections. At least she had not put in any money out of pocket.

"Look at all the mayhem they have unleashed though." Star offered him a knob of cheese. "Captain Charlie will be the first one to celebrate when they leave."

Skip's mother was a Survivor, a descendant of a deck hand from the old Isabella. He firmly believed the chaos the town was facing was a foregone conclusion.

"What were they thinking? Raking up those old memories?"

Like any sailor worth his salt, he was not ashamed of being superstitious.

"Many a times I've been saved by an unknown force," he told them. "When you're out on the open water, far away from land and man, you see things …"

He gave a sudden start and slapped his knee. Jenny and Star both stared at him, wondering what was wrong.

"I didn't go to that fancy party. Wasn't going to set foot on that ship of death, was I?" He scratched his beard. "Had to pick up a group along the coast and take 'em fishing. Corporate folks. Paid in advance and promised a big tip. Was on my way by 3 AM."

Jenny wondered if he had lost his chain of thought. She tried to steer him to what he had been saying before.

"That's 3 AM the night of the party? So you mustn't have seen the fireworks. They went off at midnight."

That must have done the trick. His eyes widened for a second and he sat down on a stool next to Star.

"I was passing that big ship over yonder when I heard a splash."

Jenny's ears perked up.

"You do mean the Isabella?"

Skip bobbed his head in assent. It had been very dark out on the water. Almost all the lights on board were extinguished. He couldn't see a thing but he waited around, in case someone had fallen in.

"Happens." He gave a shrug. "Maybe a drunk toppled over, I thought."

But there had been no alarm raised. Nor did he hear any cry for help. He was on a schedule so he went on his way and forgot about the incident.

Jenny didn't know what to make of it. Was it possible he had imagined the whole thing? She didn't know the man well enough. Maybe he was half asleep, considering it was the middle of the night.

"Would you like to stay for lunch?" she offered. "Don't get your hopes up too high though. It's just a grilled cheese sandwich and it will be the first thing I am gonna cook in the refurbished kitchen."

Skip beamed at them, telling her it was a great honor. Star offered to give him a tour. Jenny slathered the sun dried tomato pesto on thick slices of bread, added generous amounts of cheese and grilled the sandwiches in a pan.

"This needs a fancy name." Skip praised after downing a hefty bite.

Jenny had a sudden inspiration.

"How 'bout we call it Captain Skip's tomato and cheese panini? That makes it sound exotic."

The hardened old salt turned red and struggled for words.

"Charlie's right. You're a blessing, hon."

Jenny warned him she planned to experiment with it a bit more and add a few fillings.

"Serve them with salt and vinegar chips." Skip guffawed. "This is my lucky day." He stared at them in disbelief. "Never had anything named after my humble self."

Jenny talked to a few of her vendors after that and asked them to resume sending their supplies. She made a list of the few items she wanted to try the next day. Muffins and scrambled eggs, something simple. And then she would cook a slightly more elaborate lunch.

By the time she reached home, the sun was about to set and the wind had turned cooler. Star had preceded her, promising to take care of dinner. Jenny bundled up in a soft woolen blanket Betty Sue had knit for her, made herself a cup of chamomile tea and sat out in the garden, watching the sun set over the horizon. She lingered until twilight surrendered to a veil of darkness.

Star rustled up a simple meal of baked fish and vegetables, along with buttered rice and fruit crumble. Jason was going to be late and had told them he would eat out.

"How do you like the café?" They both spoke at once.

"You've worked hard for this, sweetie. Don't hesitate to tell the Cohens if you want anything changed."

Jenny shook her head. She was surprised at how perfect everything was. She was excited about the upcoming tourist season.

"We're no longer the shabby little café on the beach, are we?" she grinned. "Now if only we could make that monster coffee machine work."

They burst out laughing. Jenny admitted she was seriously considering asking Heather to take a professional course.

"Do you think she'll be willing?"

Star wasn't sure. It was hard to predict what Heather wanted.

They cleared up and Jenny urged Star to turn in early. She noted her aunt was looking tired. Maybe the stress of the past two months was finally getting to her.

Jenny laced her sneakers and forced herself to go out for a walk. But she couldn't drag her feet away from the house. Making a deal with herself, she decided to stay within sight of the house so she could go in any time she wanted. A few rounds spanning the length of it were enough. She went into the garden and sat on a bench, feeling sleepy.

A familiar pair of paws landed on her chest, just as she was nodding off.

"Tank!" she ordered him to get down. "You brute."

Adam sat down beside her, laughing to himself.

"You're hurting his feelings."

Jenny fondled the plump Labrador who had promptly flopped down at her feet. He knew how much she loved him.

Adam grew serious and told her his investigation into the Senator had yielded something.

"He was an investor in Dario's casino."

Jenny's mouth dropped open. She had not expected this. Being a part owner made the man an important stakeholder in the business.

"Are you sure? Is that allowed?"

Adam reminded her the Lombardis had somehow manipulated the legal system and were not breaking any laws. Was a Senator allowed to put money in a questionable venture like that, he couldn't say.

"It's not his money." He gave a triumphant smirk. "He sits on the board of trustees for various charities, coming from a reputed family. Man took funds from one of them and put them in the casino, hoping to make a quick profit for the charity. Then he had second thoughts and wanted it back."

He had committed a crime but how did that relate to Dario's death?

"Do you have a motive for him?"

Adam told her he might have fallen out with Dario over a lot of things. Most likely, it was regarding the handling of money. Or it could be about profit margins.

"Even if they did, would a man like the Senator come to blows with another?"

Adam agreed with her. The man would not want to dirty his hands but he could have hired anyone. Or one of his guards had acted on his orders.

Jenny wasn't convinced and told Adam that. He replied it was something, since they didn't have a lot of other leads.

"Strangling a person requires strength." Jenny mused. "Do you think I can take a look at the autopsy report?"

She fully expected him to turn her down, saying it was a confidential police document that he couldn't share with her. But he managed to surprise her.

"Sure! At this point, Jenny, I'll take whatever help you can offer."

Chapter 26

Bright sunshine streamed into the kitchen of the Boardwalk Café through the new window, putting Jenny in a cheerful mood. She hummed a tune to herself as she beat eggs in a bowl. Two pans of muffins were already in the oven. It was another dry run, this time for breakfast. She was going to stick to the usual menu for her deliveries and for the boxes people would come and pick up. But she was determined to try something more for herself and the family.

An hour later, Jenny was gently flipping a crab omelet in a new pan when Captain Charlie walked in.

"Good morning!" she chirped. "Just the man I wanted to see."

Urging him to take a seat, she plated the omelet, added some bacon and set it before him. The toaster popped and Jenny pulled the perfectly browned pieces of bread out, looking around for the butter knife.

Captain Charlie sat at the counter, barely noticing his surroundings.

"Don't let it get cold."

Jenny made a couple more omelets and went out to get Star. She had brought a few canvases from home and was placing them on the gallery floor, trying to determine the best placements.

"Are you sure these landscapes will look good enough?" Star dug into her food, doubt clouding her eyes.

Jenny assured her they were just the ticket. She ate a few bites herself and had started to butter her toast when she noticed something was amiss.

"You haven't said a word, Captain Charlie!"

He had just been moving his food around on his plate which was very unlike him.

"I made a bad call."

"Is this about that new boat?" Star asked, sharing a knowing look with Jenny.

They already knew the gist.

"It's ready to be delivered and the paperwork is almost done."

Jenny picked up on that.

"That means you can still back out."

Captain Charlie told them he could easily cancel the order but it was a technicality.

"It seemed like a good idea at the time. The casino was going to bring a lot of business. Could never have ferried all those people using just my old boat."

It had been an informal condition in his contract. Jenny pointed out it wasn't worth the paper it was written on.

"If Dario was the one you signed it with, I'd say it is void now. Why don't you let Billy or Jason handle that for you?"

Primo would most likely not stick to anything his brother had promised anyway. Look at how easily he had replaced her.

"You have a point." Captain Charlie picked up his fork, looking hopeful. "My gut feel is that ship's gonna lift anchor and sail away from our shores."

Jenny and Star both crossed their fingers and wished it would happen soon.

"Tourist season's coming up. We'll be so busy we won't have time to think of all this."

Captain Charlie began to eat and asked for fresh toast. Jenny put some bread in the toaster and excused herself. She had remembered she was to meet the Sheriff.

"I'm going to the station but I'll be back soon. Meanwhile, you can make a list of what we might cook for lunch."

She set off at a brisk pace and reached the police station a few minutes later. Adam was out on an errand but the sergeant at the desk guided Jenny to an empty room generally used for interviews. There was a folder on the table.

"Sheriff said you can take your time. Just don't take that file out of here."

Jenny thanked her, refused her offer of coffee and took a seat. She opened the folder, glad to see it contained the autopsy report Adam had promised. Skimming over the gruesome photos, she read the medical examiner's notes. Everything seemed run of the mill at first. She was making a third pass through the file when she noticed a tiny detail she had missed. There was no water in the lungs! Shocked, Jenny rushed outside to speak to Adam. But he wasn't back yet.

Deciding there was no point in hanging around, she started back for the café. Adam would call her once he found out she had been there. Engrossed in her thoughts, Jenny passed a couple of people, barely looking up.

"You tell that Betty Sue ..." a voice encroached her thoughts.

"I'm sorry?" Jenny glanced up when she sensed a presence beside her.

The woman's face was familiar. She wasn't a regular at the café but Jenny had seen her at the grocery store and at town meetings.

"We are gathering proof, you know." The woman taunted. "Tell your high and mighty friend she will never sit on a committee again. Once we show everyone how corrupt she is, the Morse name will be dust."

Jenny's mouth hung open in shock. The woman moved away before Jenny could react and say something in her friend's defence. Molly's crazy idea about the festival being used as a front for dealing drugs came to her mind. Maybe it wasn't that farfetched.

Her pace slowed as a variety of possibilities filtered through her mind. Why were so many things going wrong at the same time? The murders, the mishaps at the spring festival. It must be a coincidence though. She could not imagine a connection between the Lombardis and food truck owners who made their living cooking and selling original dishes like the lamb sliders and tacos she had tasted. One was a crime family worth billions. The others earned a pittance after hours of hard work.

But all the pandemonium they were facing had occurred only since Dario's murder. The so called short circuit and the fire on the festival grounds, the food tampering, the accusations – it was all spiraling into an impossible situation. One that might very well be the end of the simple life they lived on the island. Did the crime families have a completely different agenda? Maybe all this was just a distraction. Jenny paused to catch her breath and shook off all the crazy thoughts. She was being paranoid.

The Magnolias were sitting out on the deck, making a valiant effort to drink their coffee. Heather sprang up when she saw Jenny and offered to make her a latte.

"Just a regular coffee please. One I can fix with cream and sugar the way I like it."

"What's got your knickers in a twist?" Heather muttered and went in.

Betty Sue and Star were admiring the new deck furniture. Jenny considered telling them about the woman she had encountered and the threats she had made. Then she decided against it.

"We can put fresh flowers on every table in the summer." Molly gushed. "Nothing elaborate. Just a single rose or a bunch of daffodils, maybe."

Jenny laughed. She would need to hire another person to do all that.

Heather brought her a steaming carafe of coffee. Jenny fixed herself a cup and took a sip, trying to cherish the moment. The sun was shining, the café was looking really pretty and she was surrounded by her friends. What more could a person want?

"What do you crave for lunch? Have you given it any thought?"

They decided on Greek salad with herb grilled chicken. It was an item Jenny wanted to add to the new menu. Molly had a craving for quesadillas.

"Just cheese, with a dash of chili powder. No veggies in it please."

She went back to work but intended to come back in a couple of hours.

Heather accompanied Jenny to the kitchen. Betty Sue followed Star to the gallery room. No doubt she would give specific instructions on where each piece was to be hung.

"How was your date?" Jenny asked Heather in the kitchen. "Did you run Billy off again?"

He had a meeting in the city. Heather's phone dinged just then and her face broke into a smile.

"He's on his way back. And he'll join us for lunch."

Jenny counted on her fingers. There would be at least eight of them, the whole gang. Dare she hope Nick would pay a surprise visit?

She decided to cook for a dozen. The first batch of chicken she baked in the oven was dry. Refusing to be disheartened, Jenny adjusted the temperature and slid in another pan.

Heather kept up a monologue, talking about a range of diverse topics. It was past noon when they all gathered on deck for lunch.

"This is delicious!" Jason complimented the Greek salad. "Just perfect!"

Jenny thanked him and was about to take a bite herself when a small voice hailed her. She turned and was surprised to see the bartender girl from the Isabella standing in the doorway. There was a duffel bag slung over her shoulder.

"Hi Katie!" Jenny left the table and went to greet her. "All good?"

Everyone at the table was staring at them. Captain Charlie came up the steps from the boardwalk. The girl wilted. Jenny took her arm and led her inside.

"Guy at the pier said the café is open." Katie mumbled.

"Oh." Jenny walked to the dining room and pulled out a chair. "We're not. I'm trying to acquaint myself with the new kitchen. Just doing dry runs this week."

She saw the girl's eyes dim and realized she was hungry.

"I do need some tasters though. Would you like to volunteer?"

Without waiting for a response, she went and fixed her a plate.

"Eat." She ordered. "And be as critical as possible. I'm willing to tweak the recipe until it's crowd friendly."

Jenny leaned back in her chair and folded her arms, silent as the girl picked up a fork and began to eat. She didn't pause until she had worked through half the salad.

"The chicken is so moist," she praised. "And very flavorful. You have a winner with this salad. We don't get food like this in town."

Jenny nodded at the bag lying at the girl's feet.

"Going somewhere?"

"I was fired." The girl munched on a wedge of crispy cheese quesadilla. "And I wasn't the only one. Primo let go of a bunch of the staff. Those he thought were loyal to Dario."

Jenny wasn't surprised to hear that they had been replaced by some men who had arrived from the north, from Jersey.

Did Adam know about this, she wondered. According to the girl, some of the people who were fired had already dispersed, heading for their hometown or other jobs. The only reason she had stuck around was because she was local.

It would be almost impossible to trace all those people, Jenny mused. Her thoughts wandered and she missed half of what the girl said.

"What's that?"

"I said I'm leaving tomorrow. I signed a contract with a cruise line. My ship leaves for the Caribbean in two days. Gotta get to Fort Lauderdale before that and report on board."

This was her last chance to question the girl, Jenny realized.

"You're my last hope." She wheedled. "Are you sure you haven't remembered anything else about that night?"

The girl scrunched up her face, holding her fork aloft.

"No ma'am. If you have anything specific in mind, why don't you go ahead and ask? It might jog my memory."

Jenny thought of all the people she suspected. What if she quizzed her about them? It was a bit primitive and seemed silly.

But there was nothing to lose. She told the girl what she was thinking.

"Go ahead. Shoot."

Starting with the Senator, Jenny moved on to Peter Wilson. Those two were the ones she would put her money on. But the bartender firmly shook her head. Harry Campbell produced the same reaction.

"No point asking about the family, I guess. Primo or Bianca. They were all present at the toast."

The girl sat up with a jerk.

"Bianca. At least, I think it was her."

The girl had seen a woman go down the corridor. It had been a fleeting impression, out of the corner of her eye and it had barely registered on her mind. At the time, she had figured it was one of the guests returning to their cabin.

"But she could have gone out to that small deck!" Jenny exclaimed.

The girl gave a shrug. It was possible but she couldn't be certain.

"This is better than nothing." Jenny thanked her for coming in. "Can you talk to your friends again?" She sighed. "The slightest detail will help."

The girl promised to do what she could.

"Don't get your hopes up though. Even if they've seen anything, most of them will keep their mouths shut." She thanked

Jenny for the meal. "Dario was a generous boss but he was one of them."

Jenny stood up and hugged the girl, urging her to come visit when she was back in town. She had read between the lines and understood what the bartender was unwilling to say.

Nobody was going to risk their lives and speak against the Lombardis.

Chapter 27

Jenny kept thinking about Katie the bartender long after she joined everyone on the deck. Star nudged her after a while.

"What's the matter, sweetie? You haven't eaten much."

With a sigh, Jenny speared a few vegetables on her fork and took a bite. The dressing could be more lemony, she thought, while pondering over Katie's behavior. Had the girl been honest? Or was she just a disgruntled employee who was lashing out?

Molly called her attention to the quesadilla. It was just the way she wanted it.

"This must go on the menu. Crispy cheese quesadilla with salsa for dipping. And guacamole. It's the kind of stuff tourists like after indulging in a swim in the ocean."

Jenny promised to make a note of it. Molly was one step ahead. She pulled out a notebook from her bag and wrote it down on a page she had titled 'new menu'.

"I'll send this to you after we finish tasting everything."

"Thanks, Molls. I appreciate it."

Eating the last chunk of kalamata olive from her bowl, she suddenly stood up.

"I gotta go."

She gave Jason a quick hug and bounded down the steps to the deck before any of them had a chance to stop her.

Jenny walked to the police station at a clip. Adam must have come back by now. She couldn't beat a nagging feeling that made her believe she had missed some important detail. She needed to check Dario's file again.

"Sheriff's here." The girl at the desk pointed at his office. "You can go right in."

Adam was rifling through the same file Jenny wanted. She sat down with a thump and gave him a half hearted greeting.

"Mind if I look at that?"

"Be my guest."

Adam slid the folder toward her, watching her through hooded lids. She flipped the pages from start to end, then back again, racking her brain for the one clue that was eluding her. Frustrated, she flung it back on the table and expelled a breath.

"What am I missing?"

Adam stood up and went to a tiny refrigerator by the wall. He took two cans of soda and handed one to Jenny.

"Rough day?"

Jenny flipped the lid on her can and took a big gulp, her face set in a stony expression.

"Maybe I can cheer you up a bit." He didn't wait for her answer. "We traced the disposable phone."

"Was it ..."

"The Senator." Adam surprised her.

She had been sure it would turn out to be Peter Wilson.

Adam outlined his plan. He was going to call the Senator and have a video conference with him. It sounded better than an interrogation and saved him a long trip to the city.

"Why don't you join me? But let me take the lead, please."

Glad to be included, Jenny gave in readily.

A deputy peeked in and told Adam that everything was set up in the conference room.

"We're ready to go, Sir."

Jenny followed Adam out. They settled before the screen and put in the call.

"Here goes ..." Adam said under his breath.

Senator Worth appeared on the screen, his secretary hovering behind him.

She stayed until they conducted the basic checks and made sure either party could hear each other.

"Thank you for agreeing to this meeting, Senator." Adam began. "I know your time is valuable so I will keep this as brief as possible."

The response wasn't entirely unexpected. Senator Worth warned them to stop making baseless allegations.

"Do you deny that phone belonged to you?" Adam went on the offensive. "We have proof." He didn't stop there. "And I also know you were an investor in the whole casino project, Sir."

The man deflated like a balloon.

"Okay, okay." He held up a hand. "Dario gave me that phone. Used it to blackmail me, threaten me. That scoundrel!"

He picked up a mug on his desk and drank from it.

"And yes, I invested some money in this."

There was a long pause. Neither man said a thing. Jenny waited with bated breath, wondering who would capitulate first. It was the Senator.

He managed to shock them with his confession.

"Dario sent me a message. He wanted to meet me on that deck."

He had bombarded the Senator with a series of threats, mostly amounting to blackmail. Things escalated and the Senator punched him in the face. That's when he must have lost the cufflink.

"But he was fine when I left that deck, I swear."

Adam answered with a snort.

"Of course you will say that, Sir. No man in your position will admit he killed the guy."

The Senator's eyes turned cold. He told Adam to take whatever action he wanted.

"I have given you my full cooperation, Sheriff. Do with it what you will."

"When did you leave the deck?"

"Can't give you the exact time, but it was after midnight."

Why hadn't he returned to the party then? The Senator said he had no idea. Adam wasn't convinced.

"You'll have to do better than that, Sir."

Senator Worth leaned forward, with his elbows on his desk. Jenny noted there were circles under his eyes. The man was under stress. Was it some issue related to his work, or was the guilt of killing Dario giving him sleepless nights?

He clutched his temples and massaged them, his face ashen. There was none of the bluster that had been present when they visited him.

"Tell me why I would kill the man, Sheriff. You know I invested a bundle in this venture. It was all off the record."

Code for illegal, Jenny realized.

"The whole point was getting a high return on my investment. I could put the principal back where it came from and pocket the rest."

He had needed Dario to be alive for that.

"You have a point." Adam gave in. "I hope you are not hiding anything more, Sir. It's bound to come out sooner or later."

The screen went blank. Senator Worth had checked out before they could thank him or say anything more.

"Well, that was that!" Adam glanced at Jenny, his eyebrows raised in question. "Think he was being upfront?"

Jenny pursed her lips. She felt there was an element of truth in what the man said. But he had clearly kept them on a need to know basis, only talking around the facts they had already discovered.

"He might have left the deck when he says, Adam. But what if he sent someone else to finish the job?"

Adam agreed with her. The amount of money the Senator had invested in the ship or casino was paltry compared to his wealth. But any resulting scandal would be hard to control. If Dario was becoming a stone around his neck, he might have preferred to get rid of him.

They had not solved the case but they were closer than before. At least they knew the Senator was with Dario when he was hurt.

"You think he slipped into the water and drowned?" Jenny asked.

Adam reminded her they had not accounted for the marks around his neck. No, the man had been strangled. And if the Senator was telling the truth, he was not the one to do it.

"I'm still not willing to rule him out completely." Adam told her.

Jenny stood up, ready to leave. Before she could thank Adam for letting her stay for the interview, the door was flung open and a deputy came in.

"Trouble at the festival ground, Sir."

Adam was up in a flash and out of the door before Jenny could process what was said.

"Come on, Jenny." Adam yelled from the lobby.

She ran after him and went outside. Adam was already in a car, ready to go. He had kept the passenger door open. Lights flashed and sirens wailed. Two squad cars sped ahead.

"Get in!" Adam put his foot on the gas pedal, ordering her to put on her seat belt and sit tight.

They took off with a screech of tires. Jenny could barely focus as the car spun around corners, burning rubber. Five minutes later they arrived at the spring festival.

"Is that Betty Sue?" Jenny's heart skipped a beat at the sight facing them.

Two factions of people faced each other, held back by a few policemen. One of the women Jenny had bought food from was holding her arm aloft. Her sleeve was torn and there was mud on her clothes and face. She looked like she had suffered a fall.

The ambulance arrived just then and a team of paramedics jumped out. Jenny was relieved to see one of them head to the woman with a first aid kit.

Betty Sue, Barb Norton and Ada Newbury stood in the center between the two groups, back to back, like Charlie's Angels. Where was Heather? Why wasn't she there, keeping an eye on her grandma?

As she took in the scene, Jenny realized the two sides were talking at the top of their voices, hurling insults at each other. Adam entered the fray, heading straight for Betty Sue.

"Are you okay?" He took her arm and gently led her back to the car.

Barb followed without any objection. Ada hesitated, then joined her.

"What just happened?" Jenny quizzed.

A fight had broken out over the music that was being played. Things went awry soon.

"What's gotten into them, I don't understand!" Betty Sue wailed. "That's it. I'm shutting this festival down."

"Good call." Ada Newbury agreed with her for once. "Get these outsiders out of town by sundown, Sheriff!"

Chapter 28

Jenny couldn't say why she came back to the café. Adam was busy rounding up all the miscreants at the spring festival, booking them on various charges. One of his men had given her a ride back. They had dropped Betty Sue off at the inn first.

She sat in the dining room, trying to calm her mind and looked around. Her mind took in some details she hadn't noticed before. Star's mural itself was a masterpiece. Her aunt had highlighted a lot of special features of the region and blended them into the larger picture. Jenny had sent some photos to Mandy, their marketing expert. The young woman was coming to Pelican Cove at the earliest opportunity to check it out herself.

The café door was wide open but Jenny was not expecting anyone. So she didn't see the man until he came across her line of vision.

"Hello."

Jenny gave a start. She relaxed when she recognized the boy who had been with Katie.

"Have you been fired too?"

He answered with a shrug. It was his day off. He wasn't supposed to report back at the ship until later that evening. But he had heard about some of his friends being let go.

"Katie got the axe." He sat down when Jenny pointed at one of the empty chairs. "I warned her, many times. But she fell for Dario. Impressed by his money, I guess. None of us crew members can offer her that."

It was obvious the girl was a gold digger. She took a risk and was paying for it. Many young women in her position would probably do the same. Was it wrong, really? Jenny wasn't in a position to judge. Katie was paying the price for it now.

"She's a good kid." The waiter must have guessed what she was thinking. "He made a lot of false promises. Ones he would never have kept if he had stayed alive."

Jenny asked him the same questions she had asked the bartender. Was he sure he wasn't keeping anything from her.

"Katie will be fine." She tried to reassure him. "She's already found a new job."

This was news to him. He seemed relieved.

"Have you talked to your friends? Maybe one of them was slacking off on the job and saw something?" She patted his hand. "I'm not gonna rat them out. They have nothing to worry from me."

His ears grew red and he refused to meet her eye. Was he the one hiding something?

Jenny was quiet, letting him gather the courage to speak up.

"I saw a man." He finally admitted. "You see, I'd been working for hours without a break. I needed a smoke."

"Of course. Your feet must be killing you."

He had been on his way to the tiny deck most of the crew used for a break. The door was slightly ajar when he got there and he heard voices.

"I held off." He confessed. "One of them was the boss."

Jenny's pulse sped up. Had the boy actually witnessed the crime?

"There was a man in a dark coat with his back to the door. He and the boss were screaming at each other."

Was he sure the other man was Dario?

"Of course! I'd know that voice anywhere. And I had just come from the party. Dario was not there for the toast."

Jenny's eyebrows shot up as she heard the gist of the fight between the two men. Dario wanted the man to promise he would never come back to the casino. He had already been banned from visiting any business the Lombardis ran. There would be a price to pay if he didn't listen.

The man in the coat had to be Peter Wilson, Jenny was sure. But she said nothing to the waiter.

"Dario threatened to kill him." He finished in a burst.

Had Peter lost his temper and hurt Dario?

"He might well have," Jenny murmured.

"I don't think so. The man came out and stalked off to the elevators. Don't think he saw me. I wanted to leave but I peeped out, just to make sure the boss was okay."

Dario had been standing by the railing, staring at the shore, swearing. The waiter had hotfooted it out of there, unwilling to be caught snooping.

"What was the time, do you know?" Jenny asked.

"Ten, fifteen minutes after midnight. I left the ball room after the toast."

Jenny thanked him for opening up to her. Was he sure he wasn't keeping anything to himself?

"The Sheriff's my friend. I can put in a good word for you." She smiled. "And we just want to solve this murder."

The waiter shook his head. He had told her everything.

"I better get back to the ship. Need to find out if I still have a job."

Jenny suggested he talk to Katie. Maybe she could find him a place at the cruise line she was going to join. It would be a lot safer than the Isabella. But he might not like her interference.

"There's plenty more fish in the sea."

He threw her a boyish grin and nodded. Jenny bid him goodbye, sure he would land on his feet.

She went over everything he had said as she closed up the café. If the boy was telling the truth, Peter Wilson was in the clear. Jenny cheered at the thought. He had always been good to her and she wanted to believe he had changed.

The drive back home was quick. Star had left a note saying she was at the Bayview Inn with Betty Sue. Jenny wandered around the house, restless. Her mind was a jumble of thoughts. She needed to put the Lombardis out of it and just relax.

A message from Heather popped up on her phone. They were all meeting at the Rusty Anchor for drinks. With a fresh burst of energy, Jenny took a quick shower and dressed up. Jason arrived when she was putting on her lipstick.

"This is just what you need." He winked. "Wine and an evening with friends."

He must have gathered the troops and set the whole thing up.

They entered the familiar buzz of the Rusty Anchor pub. It had been a while since they had been there. Eddie Cotton, the proprietor, came around from the bar to greet them.

"Long time, Jenny. You're not avoiding this place, are you?"

"No, no. Of course not. I've just been busy."

He had heard great things about the Boardwalk Café and couldn't wait to come have a look.

"Has Heather been squealing? We'll have a reopening party and I wanted the new look to be a surprise."

"Not her. Some of the men who did the renovation gather here for their daily pint. It's hard not to overhear a few things."

Jenny extended an invitation right away and promised to give more details. They went to the room at the back that was usually reserved for their group. Billy was there with Heather. A bottle of wine was breathing on the table.

"Hey lovebirds!" Jenny sat and reached for the glass Billy poured for her.

Heather opened her mouth but Jenny held up a hand, warding her off.

"No talk of the Isabella or anything related to it. Off limits!" She took a sip. "And the town or the food festival."

"No wedding talk either," Heather warned.

Jason flipped the top off a bottle of beer and placed an arm around Jenny.

"We can talk of vacations we can take this summer."

Billy was all for the idea. He suggested a cruise in the Mediterranean, ending with a week at his friend's villa in Tuscany. Jenny glanced at Heather and saw the frown she was trying to hide. No doubt she wanted Billy all to herself. She would have to talk to her ex-husband and put some sense into him. Better yet, she would pass on the task to her son.

"When's our boy coming to visit?" she asked. "It's been more than a month since I saw him."

Billy had been to the city for work a few times and had managed to grab a quick lunch or two with Nick.

"No need to smother him."

"Excuse me!" Jenny sat up, her affront clear. "Don't tell me how to behave with my only son." She turned to Jason. "I almost forgot. The twins are in town. Evie is back from her tour."

Jason gave her a knowing smile.

"Are you matchmaking again, wife?"

"I gave that up long ago. Nick has always insisted he doesn't see them that way. Either of them."

A young face peeked in and said hello. It was Adam's daughter, the same one they had been talking about.

"Eddie told me you're here."

"Come in, come in." Jenny urged. "Sit and have a drink with us. Pour her some wine, Billy."

They engaged in small talk. Jenny was surprised to hear Adam's daughter planned to stay back in town.

"I'm taking some time off," she admitted.

Was she done with the army, Jenny asked. The girl wasn't sure. She was considering moving into the reserves.

"I might go back to college." She swirled the wine in her glass. "Everything's different here. Dad warned me it would be hard to adjust to civilian life."

"There's no rush." Jenny soothed. "Summer's coming and you can swim and surf all day, take a boat out on the water. Don't stress too much."

That was her plan but she also needed a job.

"Something part time to keep me busy." She laughed. "I could bus tables at the café."

Jenny suddenly had an idea. She sat up, her eyes shining wide with excitement.

"Can you handle that brutish coffee machine I let myself get talked into?"

"Probably. I'll have to take a look but I worked as a barista when I was in college."

Jenny beamed, her mouth stretching into a smile.

"You're hired!"

Chapter 29

A storm blew through Pelican Cove that night. Jenny woke to the sound of thunder, wondering what time it was. The clock on her nightstand showed it was a few minutes past two in the morning. Lightning flashed across the sky, followed by a fresh roll of thunder. Jason was fast asleep.

Jenny padded to the window and pulled herself up on the wide seat, hugging her knees close. It was dark outside but she could hear the waves crashing on the beach. The whitecaps glistened and the salt in the air felt more pronounced.

She stared at the horizon, her mind mercifully blank. Nick had sent her a message late at night, promising to be there soon. Rain started, turning into a downpour. There was a stiff breeze, cool and pleasant. Jenny stayed there for a while, then returned to bed when her eyelids began to droop.

Jason shook her awake the next morning.

"I've already snoozed the alarm twice."

She scrambled out of bed, showered and rushed to the café, wearing a cheery yellow cotton frock with butterflies on it.

Making coffee was a challenge but she managed to brew a cup for herself, wishing she hadn't allowed the workmen to take away her old coffee machine.

Her mind switched into gear as she folded the batter for muffins and cracked eggs in a bowl. She had finished packing the boxes of scrambled eggs when a thought flashed through her mind. It made her stop and reconsider everything once again.

She had been so tired the day before that her conversation with Katie's friend had barely registered on her mind. But the fog had faded and everything was clear. Forcing herself to reconstruct the timeline, Jenny went over the events of that fateful night. Everything was so clear.

Adam needed to be told right away. She picked up the kitchen phone and glanced at the clock on the wall. It was forty minutes past six. Realizing it was a bit early to call him, she decided to finish her breakfast deliveries. It was two minutes to eight when she parked her car outside the police station.

"Sheriff's in." The desk sergeant nodded.

Jenny knocked and pushed the door open, barely waiting for a response.

"I've got it."

Adam was silent while she laid out her theory. She didn't pause until she was done, then looked up to meet his stony expression.

"You don't believe me."

"Let me handle this, Jenny. Go back to the café. And please promise you will stay away from the Isabella. Do not put yourself in any danger under any circumstances. Do you promise?"

Miffed at his lukewarm response, Jenny gave a stiff nod and left, slamming the door on her way out. Back at the café, she went on a chopping frenzy. She was going to cook all the old favorites that day.

Star arrived and took in the scene, raising her eyebrows but saying nothing.

"How can I help, sweetie?"

Jenny bid her to call everyone and tell them they were expected for lunch at the café.

"This is not an invite, then?"

"Hunh?" Jenny looked up with a frown.

She saw the twinkle in her aunt's eyes and finally gave a grudging smile.

"I'm in a bad mood. Can you tell?"

Star listened to her harangue about Adam. She advised her to be patient.

The Magnolias arrived for coffee. Heather had started to fiddle with the machine when Adam's daughter came in, her face alight.

"Let me take care of that. Just let me know what you'd like."

Heather asked for a caramel macchiato with soy milk. Jenny told her they didn't have that.

"Just make cappuccinos for everyone," Jenny told Evie. "I baked a batch of chocolate chip cookies with marshmallows. Those are your favorites, aren't they?"

They sat on the deck, nibbling on cookies. Betty Sue was busy knitting a blanket in yellow and brown. She sat with her back to the boardwalk which was very unusual.

"This is good coffee." Molly looked around the table. "Did you hear the storm last night?"

Conversation around the table was stilted, Heather glued to her phone and Jenny gazing at the ocean, tapping her toe impatiently. Star was the only one who seemed happy.

"So we're having shrimp po'boys for lunch?"

"And sticky wings, pimento cheese sandwiches, turkey chili and cannolis." Jenny rattled off the list.

Molly thought it was too ambitious. Jenny pinned her with a glare.

"I only have a few days before the café reopens."

Adam's daughter came out, waving her phone before them.

"Dad wants you at the police station, Jenny."

All the eyes swung toward her, expecting her to erupt. Adam had no right to order her around. But Jenny surprised all of them.

She was out of her chair in a flash and down the steps to the boardwalk before anyone could say a word. Five minutes later, she swarmed into the police station.

Adam was at the front desk, waiting for her.

"We got her." He beamed. "I'm about to question her now. You can watch us through the glass."

Jenny opened her mouth to thank him.

"I'd rather not have you in there now. We'll see how things go."

He took Jenny to an alcove she had not seen before. There was a small chair wedged in there, in front of a one way glass. Jenny chose to stand.

Adam entered the room. One of his deputies stood in a corner. The woman sitting at the table filled the room with her presence. Wearing a white strapless dress that clung to her curves, her lips painted a vivid shade of red, a pair of sunglasses perched on her head, Bianca Lombardi looked like she didn't have a care in the world. She might as well be lounging on a yacht in the middle of the ocean, sipping champagne.

"Are you going to tell us how you did it?" Adam began.

There was no response. Undeterred, he launched into a minute by minute account of how things had unfolded aboard the Isabella on the day of the big party.

Jenny knew some of it was just a theory at that point. It would remain so until Bianca validated it.

"You knew the Senator was heavily invested in the casino. You sent him a message from Dario's phone, asking to meet on that out of the way deck just before midnight."

It had served a dual purpose. Dario had not been present for the toast, drawing his father's disapproval.

Bianca's expression remained inscrutable. Adam continued.

"We have interviewed Senator Worth a few times. He told us they met on that deck around midnight. Both were confused about why they were there. The Senator was angry, thinking Dario was playing games with him, trying to intimidate him." He paused.

There was no response from Bianca.

"There was a fight, of course. The Senator punched Dario and lost his cufflink on the deck. You couldn't have planned it better. Did you know the Senator had a short fuse? How could you be sure that he and your baby brother would push each other around?"

Jenny was watching Bianca like a hawk. She saw her eyelids flicker. A hint of a smirk appeared on her face but she said nothing.

"It was very smart," Adam went on. "Framing the Senator like that. You planned to go there and finish the job."

But she hadn't anticipated every possibility. Wilson muddied the waters by going out there. A witness heard him argue with Dario, then saw him leave.

Adam leaned forward with his elbows on the table, staring at Bianca.

"Dario Lombardi was still alive at that point."

There was an answering shrug. Was Bianca getting impatient or was she just bored?

"You went there next." Adam smiled. "Don't even try to deny it because you were spotted in that tiny passage, on your way to the deck. It was about fifteen minutes past midnight." His voice hardened. "That's when you killed him. I don't know how you managed that. A frail woman like you."

Jenny crossed her fingers. She realized Adam was baiting the woman. She saw Bianca's fingers curl and knew it was the right move.

Adam went on to say she must have hid the body on the deck. She returned to the party, acting like nothing had happened. Then she went back to the deck around three in the morning and pushed the body overboard.

Bianca was looking pale. There was an expression of shock on her face. She had probably not expected them to know when she dumped the body in the water.

"What did you think?" Adam laughed. "That you would start a rumor about how much your poor brother drank that night? That he slipped and fell into the water?" He shook his head and chuckled. "It's not easy to fool the medical examiner. The police knew right away that Dario did not die from drowning."

There was a shrill cry. Jenny shrank back, taken unawares. Adam was cool as a cucumber.

"Of course I killed him." Bianca's eyes flashed fire. "The little brat! He was like a parasite, spending Daddy's money all his life. Then he has this silly business idea all of a sudden. As if there aren't enough casinos on cruise ships. Bah!"

Jenny sat down.

"Dad forced me to put all my money in the Isabella. Primo too. I come here and what do I see? Gross mismanagement. He ran through all our funds and took more from the Senator. I begged him to let me run the show. But no. I'm just a woman. What do I know?"

She raved and ranted and came to the point where she faced her brother on the deck. This was the most critical part, Jenny knew.

"He insulted me before the whole family. But I was going to reason with him one last time. But would he listen? There was a piece of rope lying on the deck. He laughed when I swung it around his neck and began to squeeze. Said I wasn't strong enough!"

She hadn't planned the rest. Bianca heard footsteps in the passage outside and realized how vulnerable she was. Shoving the body in a dark corner, she returned to the party and played it by ear. It was almost three when she had a chance to go back there. It had not been planned to the minute.

Adam told her she would have to sign a confession. But they had it all on tape. He just wanted the Isabella gone from their shore.

Jenny thought of Philomena Ryder. Had Adam forgotten her? Incensed, she burst inside, attacking Bianca with a barrage of questions.

"Why did you send Quinn? He's more your henchman than a private investigator, I bet. Did you really think I would be taken in by his flattery?"

Bianca's neck swung between the two of them. She let out a raucous laugh.

"Is this how you run things, Sheriff? Let this shrew call the shots?"

Quinn was a loyal soldier. He had always done anything she asked him to.

"Including murdering a poor old woman?" Jenny tensed. "She had no idea you were guilty."

Bianca spread her hands wide. In their business, they didn't take risks. It's what she had learned at her father's knee. Loose ends were a liability.

"Let me put it this way. Loose lips sink ships. That woman was the first person I saw after I went back to the party. She was standing outside the elevator, drinking the free champagne, no doubt planning to sneak around and have a peep at the cabins."

Was that all? Jenny felt her eyes grow moist.

"She asked how much my dress cost. Then she told me I'd missed the fireworks." Bianca folded her arms together. "That woman could easily shake my alibi."

Philomena had never mentioned the incident. She had probably been tipsy and didn't remember it at all. But she was a loose end. The grand party on the ship had proved fatal for her.

"So you ordered your man Quinn to murder her?" Adam questioned.

Bianca answered with a shrug. He took care of things for her. There was no need to spell it out.

Jenny staggered outside, still in a daze. Her legs wobbled and she collapsed in the chair, unable to support herself. The blood rushed in her ears and Philomena's cheerful face filled her vision. She'd been full of zest, taking great pleasure in something as simple as a muffin.

None of this would have happened if the Lombardis hadn't anchored their ship off Pelican Cove. The Isabella's curse was real after all.

Chapter 30

Spring firmly arrived in Pelican Cove, making its presence known. The cherry trees were beginning to blossom. Colorful flowers spilled over beds and boxes in gardens and along Main Street. Jenny had planted masses of daffodils around the periphery of the Boardwalk Café. They provided a lovely contrast to the freshly painted white and stone building, bobbing in the brilliant sunshine and light breeze.

To everyone's relief, peace had settled after the spring festival shut down and the food trucks went back to wherever they had come from. Everyone expected the Isabella to vanish after Bianca's confession. But the Lombardis turned out to be thick skinned. The ship remained anchored offshore. Car loads of guests arrived and were ferried using some fancy boats the Lombardis owned. As expected, Captain Charlie had been left in the lurch.

The resentment that had simmered in the town reached a crescendo. A town meeting was called and people unanimously voted to drive the ship away from their shore. But they had no control over the Isabella, since it was anchored a certain distance away from the town. Stronger measures were needed.

A three person delegation of Jenny, Billy and Jason took a trip to the city and met Senator Worth. They requested him to use his influence and put the screws on Lombardi.

"My hands are tied." He flashed a condescending smile. "From a legal standpoint, you don't have any rights here."

His advice was to ride it out. The Lombardis would leave when they grew tired of the region.

Jenny had anticipated this. Billy brought up some of the unpleasant facts they had learned about the Senator. That did the job.

"Can't believe we just blackmailed a Senator!" Jenny exclaimed when they stepped out of his antebellum mansion and started back home.

"It's all give and take for these people." Billy laughed. "He can't afford a scandal in an election year."

Jenny wondered if the Senator had learned a lesson. Would he still misuse funds at his disposal, hoping to make a quick buck?

"Do birds fly?" Jason quipped, giving her a wink.

"Don't be naïve." Billy smirked from the back seat.

They went home and Jenny plunged into testing more recipes and planning the party.

The day of the grand reopening brought fair weather. As promised, Jenny had invited all her friends and given an open invitation to her loyal customers. Almost the whole town was expected to turn up for the day long celebration. Jenny glowed with happiness as she stood by the door, flanked by Jason and her son Nick, welcoming the guests. Heather and Molly had been put in charge of the food. Star and Betty Sue held court on the newly polished deck, swapping stories from their salad days with the other old ladies.

Billy and Captain Charlie mingled through the crowd, urging everyone to try all the food.

Large buffet tables had been set up in the dining area. Jenny had been given the choice of cooking just three dishes. She made her pimento cheese dip which was a must, considering their location. Cookies and cannolis made up the trio. A catering firm had been hired to feed the crowd and barbecue was on the menu, along with burgers, hot dogs and fried chicken. Heather suggested they engage one of the food trucks, the one that made the delicious tacos, but she had been warned to stop making trouble.

"This is a marketing triumph." Mandy spoke, eating pulled pork with a plastic fork. "Everyone is taking pictures by the mural. It's going to make you famous, Jenny!"

A TV crew was expected in a couple of weeks, a famous chef coming along to do a feature on the café. Jenny hoped the new menu would be up by then.

Nick had taken three days off and arrived at midnight the day before.

"I drove here straight from work." He wrapped Jenny in a tight hug. "And I'm starving!"

A plate of leftover roast chicken was fixed for him. Jenny made a pot of cheesy pasta to accompany it.

"Evie's in town. You can meet her tomorrow."

Nick acted surprised but Jenny wasn't fooled.

"You knew she was back! Did you two meet in town?"

"The twins and I met for a drink once," he admitted. "She's at a loose end."

"Not anymore." Jenny told him Evie was going to be a barista at the Boardwalk Café. "I'm sure it's temporary. That girl's meant for greater things."

Nick said nothing. Jenny guessed he was keeping something from her but she let it slide. Maybe Evie would open up on her own.

She noted the silent glances passing between her son and Evie as the day of the party progressed. The café and the deck were packed and people stood around on the beach, sipping tea, sampling food and chatting.

Jenny spotted Adam on the boardwalk and waved.

"It's about time. Thank you for coming!"

"Finally got done with the paperwork," he sighed, his gaze roving over the crowd. "Looks like the entire Eastern Shore is here to wish you well Jenny."

"Just Pelican Cove." She blushed.

Evie came by with a tray. She had been working hard, turning out samples of fancy coffee based drinks. Some of the locals had never heard of them and they were entranced.

"Care for an affogato, Dad?"

Adam took the paper cup she offered and thanked her. Jenny saw a frown line appear between his brows.

"Evie ..." Adam cleared his throat.

She was gone before he could say anything else.

"All well?" Jenny murmured.

She saw Evie take off her apron and leave, going down the boardwalk. Nick's eyes locked on her. He excused himself and followed her.

"I'm a bit concerned," Adam said.

"Do you object to her working at the café?" Jenny's eyebrows shot up. "It's just temporary."

"Is it?" Adam followed her to the grill and picked up a plate. "I'm not so sure."

Jenny bristled with indignation. What was he saying?

"You think working as a barista is beneath her. Is that it? Let me tell you, Sheriff. It's honest work. And I'm really proud of Evie for offering to help."

Adam looked stricken.

"Will you always misunderstand me, Jenny?"

He stood there, holding a plate loaded with fried chicken and corn on the cob. At that moment, he was just a concerned parent.

"Was Evie injured in the line of duty?"

Adam gave a shrug and exhaled loudly.

"In a manner of speaking. She needs help, Jenny. But she won't listen. Will you talk to her?"

**

Enjoying solving mysteries in Pelican Cove? Stay tuned for more in the next book in the series.

Acknowledgements

I am so grateful you decided to read this book. Many thanks to all my readers for loving the Pelican Cove series.

Thank you to my beta readers and editor who painstakingly wade through early drafts to point out the flaws and errors. And each and every one of you who writes in or likes, comments, shares on social media. Your action helps others like you find my books. I really appreciate it.

As always, a big thank you to my wonderful family for their unwavering support. They fuel me with coffee and food and take care of the mundane stuff, allowing me to focus on writing the next book.

Books by Leena Clover
Pelican Cove Cozy Mystery Series

Strawberries and Strangers – Pelican Cove Cozy Mystery Book 1

https://www.amazon.com/dp/B07CSW34GB/

Cupcakes and Celebrities – Pelican Cove Cozy Mystery Book 2

https://www.amazon.com/dp/B07CYX5TNR

Berries and Birthdays – Pelican Cove Cozy Mystery Book 3

https://www.amazon.com/gp/product/B07D7GG8KV

Sprinkles and Skeletons – Pelican Cove Cozy Mystery Book 4

https://www.amazon.com/dp/B07DW91NKG

Waffles and Weekends – Pelican Cove Cozy Mystery Book 5

https://www.amazon.com/dp/B07FRJ1FC1/

Muffins and Mobsters – Pelican Cove Cozy Mystery Book 6

https://www.amazon.com/dp/B07GRBCZG8/
Parfaits and Paramours – Pelican Cove Cozy Mystery Book 7
https://www.amazon.com/dp/B07K5G2DDJ
Truffles and Troubadours – Pelican Cove Cozy Mystery 8
https://www.amazon.com/dp/B07N6FQTK2/
Sundaes and Sinners– Pelican Cove Cozy Mystery 9
https://www.amazon.com/dp/B07PXYPNG5/
Croissants and Cruises– Pelican Cove Cozy Mystery 10
https://www.amazon.com/dp/B082L2W6V2
Pancakes and Parrots– Pelican Cove Cozy Mystery 11
https://www.amazon.com/dp/B082H1DJ42
Cookies and Christmas – Pelican Cove Cozy Mystery 12
https://www.amazon.com/dp/ B08FB1TTCJ
Popsicles and Poisons
Biscuits and Butlers
https://www.amazon.com/dp/B09HGZ9FTH
Pies and Pariahs
https://www.amazon.com/dp/B0DMS2KRXL
Flans and Felonies
https://www.amazon.com/dp/B0DVZH512Y
Cannolis and Casinos
https://www.amazon.com/dp/B0F9STJXPX

Dolphin Bay Cozy Mystery Series

Raspberry Chocolate Murder – Dolphin Bay Cozy Mystery Book 1
https://www.amazon.com/dp/B07VVQDGPN
Orange Thyme Death – Dolphin Bay Cozy Mystery Book 2
https://www.amazon.com/dp/B07W226H71
Apple Caramel Mayhem – Dolphin Bay Cozy Mystery Book 3
https://www.amazon.com/dp/B07YN35K2Y
Cranberry Sage Miracle – Dolphin Bay Cozy Mystery Book 4
https://www.amazon.com/dp/B08538MP3Z
Blueberry Chai Frenzy- Dolphin Bay Cozy Mystery Book 5
https://www.amazon.com/dp/B08CTC9M5G
Mango Chili Cruiser
https://www.amazon.com/dp/B08XY1D5Q2
Strawberry Vanilla Peril
https://www.amazon.com/dp/B08XY368ZP
Cherry Lime Havoc
https://www.amazon.com/dp/B098P6M1S7
Pumpkin Ginger Bedlam
https://www.amazon.com/dp/B09JYHGS8P

Meera Patel Cozy Mystery Series
Gone with the Wings – Meera Patel Cozy Mystery Book 1
https://www.amazon.com/dp/B071WHNM6K
A Pocket Full of Pie - Meera Patel Cozy Mystery Book 2

https://www.amazon.com/dp/B072Q7B47P/

For a Few Dumplings More - Meera Patel Cozy Mystery Book 3

https://www.amazon.com/dp/B072V3T2BV

Back to the Fajitas - Meera Patel Cozy Mystery Book 4

https://www.amazon.com/dp/B0748KPTLM

Christmas with the Franks – Meera Patel Cozy Mystery Book 5

https://www.amazon.com/gp/product/B077GXR4WS/

British Cozy Mystery Series

Murder at Buxley Manor

https://www.amazon.com/dp/B0BVG7V2DY

Murder at Castle Morse

https://www.amazon.com/gp/product/B0BX8XB27G

Murder at Ridley Hall

https://www.amazon.com/dp/B0CBQCSFZF

Meg Butler Cruise Cozy Series

Sail Away Patsy

https://www.amazon.com/dp/B09XHY3PBG

Bingo Bashed

https://www.amazon.com/dp/B0BZKK6FWX

Suite Knife

Casino Foil

https://www.amazon.com/dp/B0D187JVZ3

Printed in Dunstable, United Kingdom